Murder at the Rocket Club

P. C. JAMES

VINCI
BOOKS

Vinci Books

vinci-books.com

Published by Vinci Books Ltd in 2026

1

A CIP catalogue record for this book is available from the British Library.
Paperback ISBN: 9781036713683
The EU GPSR authorised representative is Logos Europe, 9 rue Nicolas
Poussion, 17000 La Rochelle, France
contact@logoseurope.eu

By P.C. James

Miss Riddell Cozy Mysteries

Chapter One

NEWCASTLE-UPON-TYNE, ENGLAND

3 October 1957

Pauline Riddell looked from her office window across the rooftops of the factory toward where she knew the River Tyne flowed through the city and out to sea, about ten miles away. It was a grey day, made gloomier by the coal smoke rising from a thousand chimneys: from the ever-moving passenger trains crossing the High-Level Bridge, the smaller engines hauling freight from ships docked in the Tyne, and, of course, from the funnels of the ships themselves.

Down below, muffled by brick walls and distance, came the thump of heavy machinery and the whine of lighter tools cutting and grinding, a rhythm not unlike a pop song, perhaps something by Lonnie Donegan's Skiffle Group or Elvis Presley being *All Shook Up*. Though she was far above all that din, Pauline felt as though she had vertigo—she could fall just as fast as she had risen. She shivered as a sudden flurry of rain rattled against the window. Autumn in the sooty city was never appealing.

She smiled. What was appealing was her new office and her own secretary. Well, private to her and the three men in her department. Her success with numbers, especially her knack for spotting the dishonest ones, had carried her from the typing pool to private secretary of an influential Director, then through university sponsorship and a year's sabbatical to qualify as an accountant. Four years later, that journey had ended with her in a senior position, her own department (small though it was), and her own secretary. Even better, from the grimy, soot-flecked window she could look down into the factory yard and see her car in her very own parking space.

She chuckled at the sight of her old Austin among the Jaguars, Rovers, Rileys, and other late-model cars beloved by upper management. A new car was high on her list, once she'd found her feet. Yet she had a sudden urge to keep the Austin, so she would stand out: a tangible reminder of her meteoric rise. Shaking her head, she returned to her desk. Of course, she couldn't; it would also suggest she wasn't serious.

As a woman in senior management, Pauline felt keenly the need to demonstrate competence. One reason she still drove the Austin was because her first month's salary had gone on proper clothes. Three new suits, black, dark grey, and navy, each with stockings, shoes, and blouses to match. Men didn't wear colours, and nor did Pauline Riddell. Not at the office. In truth, though, the attire suited her perfectly. She had always been a "serious" person. "Old head on young shoulders" was what people had said of her as a child, and she still prided herself on it.

Even her desk proclaimed seriousness: solid oak, green leather top, an executive's desk. She ran her fingertips across the leather surface, as she so often did. It comforted her to know she had arrived. And yet the lack of work her department had been given troubled her.

A discreet knock at the door interrupted her thoughts.

"Come in," Pauline called.

Brenda Cuthbert entered with a buff folder and a determined expression. "The Managing Director's office sent this out. It's for the meeting this afternoon."

Pauline scanned the contents. Again, nothing for her department. She grimaced, itching for work; her staff were restless too. "Maybe something will come up in the meeting," she told Brenda, who had correctly read her expression and looked equally disappointed.

"Maybe," Brenda agreed. A month had passed since they'd been installed in their offices, and they had hoped the new "Forensic Auditing" department would be given a serious project at once. It seemed their creation had been more in hope than in need.

Pauline brightened, realizing she needed to rally her troops. "Year-end accounting will begin in earnest soon enough. Something is bound to come out of that."

Brenda smiled and nodded before leaving. But Pauline knew she was worried too. Brenda had left a steady post to take this one, and if the department were closed as quickly as it had opened, the consequences would sting. Her children needed school uniforms, among other things, hard to provide on her husband's salary alone. Prices were climbing everywhere.

Pauline laid the papers on her desk and began reading. The meeting wasn't chiefly about accounting, but sales, revenues, and costs were part of it and perhaps that was why she had been invited. Someone at the top suspected something, and Forensic Auditing was expected to find out.

Yet nothing in the documents pointed to trouble. Perhaps the presentations would. She hoped so.

That evening, she left the meeting more hopeful than she had entered. Each department head had presented progress and budgets, yet Pauline spotted discrepancies. Small, but real. She asked questions and received the answers she expected -- too neat, too ready. For the first time she glimpsed why her department existed.

Still smiling, she reached her office and snatched up the ringing telephone. Out of breath, she announced, "Riddell."

"I've pencilled in a meeting in my office for nine tomorrow morning," said the Managing Director. "We need to talk."

Pauline's smile widened. She beamed. "I'll be there. We have a lot to talk about."

He bade her goodnight and rang off. Still grinning, Pauline considered which files to take home. She had plenty of reading ahead.

By the time she emerged into the dark, she was laden with files and binders beyond what her stuffed leather brief-case could hold. The case, her parents' gift when she passed her final exams, pleased her greatly. They had been disappointed when she left their rural world for the (to them) sinister world of industry and finance. The case, embossed with her initials, had been both acknowledgement and farewell. It was kindly meant, and she felt that.

She was juggling her burdens at her car when a figure in raincoat and trilby stepped from the shadows.

"You frightened me, Neville," she exclaimed, clutching at her slipping binders.

Neville Halliday caught the largest before they spilled.

"Sorry," he said with a grin, "but I wanted to speak to you away from the offices."

Like Pauline, Neville was something of a rising star. Both were still in their twenties, holding posts that would once have been reserved for men with decades more service.

Once her binders were piled on the car roof, Pauline unlocked the door. "What about?" she asked.

"I have some invoices and receipts I think you should see," Neville said, handing her the last binder.

"Why not during office hours?" she asked, puzzled.

"Because they're from the Rocket Club."

The "Rocket Club" -- now formally the Rocket Department -- was the company's attempt to enter the new world of missiles and reduce dependence on conventional arms. Neville had persuaded the Board, and he now headed a small team with a modest budget. But it was a wrench for such a traditional firm. Both managers and workers had invested their lives in the old products, and even a hint of change unsettled them. There had already been small acts of sabotage. Perhaps what Neville carried was a more subtle version.

"Can I give you a lift home?" Pauline asked. She disliked talking shop in the damp October darkness of the car park.

"I hoped you would," Neville said cheerfully. "We poor engineers have to travel by bus."

Pauline laughed as she unlocked her car. "Your Jowett Javelin isn't a car?"

"Not one I can park at work anymore," Neville admitted, climbing in.

"That's still going on?" she asked. "I thought it had been stopped."

"Security can't watch everything," he said. "Our

5

possible new product may employ many in future, but right now it unsettles the old hands."

Pauline started the Austin. The engine coughed and spluttered into life. She smiled at Neville's grimace. "I'm going to buy a new one soon."

He raised an eyebrow at the clunk of the gears. "Leave it with me on Saturday, I'll give it some attention. You might get another year out of it."

"Is it that bad?" she teased.

"No, just neglected." He grinned.

As they left the factory gates, Pauline asked, "What do you want me to look at?"

Neville produced a folder from his coat and placed it on the dashboard. "These went through purchasing, supposedly for the rocket project. But we didn't order them, and we never received the parts."

"Mistake?" Pauline suggested.

He shook his head. "I checked, quietly like. And I phoned the supplier. They said it was a regular order. The only mistake was that the paperwork came to me."

"Then it should be easy to find who placed the order and approved payment."

Neville gave a short laugh. "It is. And that's the problem. On paper, I placed the order and paid the bill as head of the Rocket Department."

"But you didn't," Pauline said flatly.

"Exactly. That's why I'm here." He pointed to the next street. "This is me."

Pauline pulled up outside a Victorian semi. Unlike the east end, the brickwork here glowed red in the light of her car's headlamps, spared the soot blowing across the city.

Neville got out. "You will look into it?"

Pauline frowned. Petty fraud seemed small work

compared with what the MD had just hinted at. Yet at lunchtime she would have leapt at the chance.

"We will," she said. "But it has to go alongside the work the boss is setting us. I can't promise speed."

His expression grew grave. "So long as you're quick enough to keep me from being fired for theft, I'll be satisfied." He bade her goodnight and shut the door.

"I'll take you up on that offer to look at my car," Pauline called.

He turned, grinned in the porch light, and nodded.

Pauline drove away, her mind already on the evening's reading. She had a vague unease that Neville's documents might be part of something much, much larger.

Chapter Two

SPUTNIK IN SPACE

Yesterday's rain and cold had led to the city waking to a thick fog swirling up from the river and spilling out into the streets. Pauline crept slowly to work, her car in a long line of similarly creeping traffic. She was growing nervous as time went by, knowing she was going to be late. It was true she was now a senior manager, but she couldn't shake the training of four years punching a clock each morning. Pauline suspected she never would. It wasn't in her nature to be late or workshy.

There had been a time, shortly after solving some murders, when she'd considered leaving her secretarial career to become a private detective. Her friend, Inspector Ramsay, had advised against that, saying it "wasn't a nice occupation for anyone, let alone a young woman." Pauline smiled; she could still hear him in his distinctive mix of Scots and northern English. He'd been right, of course, and her boss of those days -- whom she'd helped before becoming his private secretary -- had supported her in the years that followed. He was now Managing Director, and his decisions regarding the establishment of a Forensic Audit office and a Rocket Project were, to Pauline, among the brightest hopes for the old, slowly fading company. Why others couldn't see it, she found harder to understand.

Arriving in the yard, she parked quickly and almost ran to her office to prepare for her meeting.

Neville, after abandoning the slowly crawling bus and walking the rest of the way, was on time for work. His first stop, after hanging his coat in his small, cluttered office, was the shed where his department's latest iteration of the rocket lay on cradles, ready to be worked on. It was twenty feet long and about three feet in diameter -- larger than the missile planned as a final product, but necessarily so in order to carry the equipment monitoring its launch flight. As yet, the rocket had no official name. The men called it *Flying Geordie*, 'Geordie' being the name given to anyone born in Newcastle-upon-Tyne.

"Are we ready?" Neville asked Evan Scott, his senior tradesman and lathe operator.

"Ready as we'll ever be," Evan replied with a shrug. "The rocket's ready. Whether the sparkies are finished with the electrics or not is another matter."

Neville grinned. There was never much love lost between the mechanical and electrical trades. "Ron says they will be, now we have that new transistor package. They're fitting it today."

Evan grunted. Neville assumed this was a good sign and left him to go in search of his electrical boffin, Ron Gaude. Ron was examining the new board that had arrived the previous afternoon with an intense stare.

"Is it all right?" Neville asked.

"Who can tell?" Ron replied. "These modern devices aren't like vacuum tubes, where you can see inside."

"But the connections are right?" Neville persisted, correctly interpreting the older man's deep distrust of anything modern as peevishness, not genuine concern.

"Oh, aye. They're right enough," Ron replied. "Everything will be ready for the roll-out this afternoon."

"Tomorrow will be exciting," Neville said. Today, the rocket was to be transported from the factory to the testing site at Spadeadam, about forty miles away. Launches so far had been unsatisfactory for a number of reasons, the latest being electrical controls, hence the new transistor package, especially created for the rocket.

"The transport is already in the yard," Neville pointed out.

Ron nodded. "I saw it. We'll be ready when I say we're ready. You can have it done right, or right now. You choose."

"You know the answer," Neville responded sharply. Sometimes Ron bordered on insubordinate, and it bothered him. "Just be ready for the move at one o'clock."

Nodding to Ron, Neville headed for his office. It bothered him that he'd let Ron get under his skin, but he knew why: the last launch hadn't been a success. The resulting Board meeting, where he'd had to explain the failure, convinced him he had only one more chance. Tomorrow was that launch, and today was the most nerve-wracking part of the journey. The long flatbed trailer winding through narrow roads to the launch site provided many opportunities for accidents -- or sabotage. He planned to ride on the trailer with the rocket the whole way.

Pauline left her boss's office beaming. Her own suspicions were confirmed by her boss's better-informed ones, and she had a briefcase full of confidential files to examine.

Before she'd even reached her office door, she could hear excitement rising through the stairwells and even outside in the yard. Puzzled, she stepped through the door into her outer office, where even Brenda was on her feet, unable to be still.

"The Russians have put a satellite into space!" Brenda cried, her whole body shivering in excitement. "Our boys had better get their skates on."

"What are you saying?" Pauline asked, passing through the outer office and dumping her armful of documents on her desk.

"What satellite?"

"Sputnik," Brenda said, following her into the room.

"But what is it?" Pauline asked. Her whole life these past four years had been enveloped by accounting studies, and nothing Brenda was saying made any sense.

"It's a satellite," Brenda said. "It's up there." She pointed through the window to the sky.

"Why? What for?" Pauline asked, though she suspected she'd need Neville to explain if she was to make sense of it.

"Being communists," Brenda said, "probably to spy on us. They probably want to watch Flying Geordie roll out this afternoon."

Pauline couldn't help feeling that if the Russians had put a 'satellite' into space, they'd hardly be interested in a rocket going only a few miles up—but she didn't say so.

"Where did you hear this?" Pauline asked.

"It was on the news," Brenda cried. "Did you miss it?"

"The MD and I were too busy to listen to the radio," Pauline retorted, though she couldn't help feeling the news eclipsed all the intense discussions they'd had. Some accounting issues did seem small beer compared with humans placing something into orbit. "I'll phone Neville and see what he has to say."

Neville's line was busy, however. She guessed every Director in the company was trying to get the first sensible thoughts they'd hear that day, ready to repeat them at any meeting the MD called. After five failed attempts, Pauline decided to go to his office directly. It was almost lunchtime anyway.

When she arrived at the rocket shed, the giant trailer was being backed into the open doors. With all the excitement, she'd forgotten this was the day for the move to the testing site. Throngs of people stood in a circle around the vehicle while Neville and his crew shooed them away. Neville looked harassed, and understandably so. It seemed half the factory had come out for an early lunch to watch.

"Lot of fuss for something that will flop again," a voice muttered at her shoulder. Pauline turned to see Bob Wallace expertly rolling a cigarette. He sealed it with a lick, raised it to his lips, and lit it with a flourish.

"With today's news," Pauline replied, "I'm not sure it will matter if it flies. The government will fund the work. The Russians in space must be a shock to many governments around the world."

"The Yanks'll be fast after them," Bob said. "We should concentrate down here on Earth. Let those looneys chase each other in space."

Pauline grinned. "Listen to the excitement, Bob. Everyone out here is ready to join the race."

Bob shook his head. "They're excited because the news

coincides with this next test. Nobody else in the country cares tuppence for satellites or rockets. They want jobs, homes, food on the table, and a bit left at the end of the week for pleasure."

Pauline laughed. "I expect you're right. I must say the news didn't mean much to me either. I can't see what use a satellite could be. But Neville's right, we need to branch out into rockets. They're the future of warfare, and if we hope to be in that future, we need this rocket to work."

Their conversation ended when the rocket's nose began sliding onto the trailer. Even the crowd, which had grown now it was past twelve and official lunch break, fell silent as the silvery cylinder locked in place. Pauline couldn't hear, but she felt the collective sigh of relief.

The truck inched forward, Neville standing alongside. Slowly, it crept to the gates.

Pauline pushed through to the trailer and called, "Neville, we must talk when you get back."

"I hope we launch later this afternoon, so it'll have to be tomorrow," Neville replied.

Pauline waved as the trailer began turning to exit. "Tomorrow morning then."

Neville grinned, gave her a thumbs-up, and sat down on the flatbed, leaning back against the rocket. Two police motorbikes fell in behind as the convoy left the factory. People spilled into the street to watch until it was out of sight.

Pauline turned away, heading back toward her office, when she noticed through the Staff Canteen windows three people she wouldn't have expected together: Senior Manager Morris Fenham, disgruntled electrical engineer Ethel Lambton, and Violet Paisley, the office's blonde bombshell. An odd grouping -- and why weren't they outside watching the rocket? Normally, Pauline wouldn't have given it more than a second's thought. But Neville had handed her those documents last night.

Back in her office, Pauline began reviewing the new papers. One caught her eye because it seemed familiar, and she sifted through her briefcase for the papers Neville had given her the night before. She wasn't mistaken: the same pattern again. Orders placed and paid for, but the stores showed no record of the goods received.

It was dark before she finished. Rising from her chair, she looked out the window. The moon and even some stars shone in a clear sky. She wondered if one of those "stars" was Sputnik and, if so, what it was watching.

"Maybe Flying Geordie will knock you off your perch tomorrow," Pauline told Sputnik sternly. "That'll teach you to stare in at other people's windows."

Chapter Three

THE LAUNCH

It was late afternoon, only an hour since the rocket had been placed on the launch pad, and Neville's eyes flicked between the launch console and the rocket outside, less than a mile away. His heart was racing, every nerve twitching. He realized he wasn't breathing and forced himself to gulp down air.

The technician beside him grinned. "The waiting's the worst."

Neville nodded. He had spoken to launch-site management before leaving the factory, reminding them that a brief window in the weather meant the launch should happen soon after arrival and final checks. They had agreed and begun alerting neighbouring airfields, towns, villages, and emergency services. Now Flying Geordie was ready to go — but the final word had not yet been given. Darkness was already closing in, and soon it would be too late. The weather overnight and tomorrow was forecast to be poor.

The phone rang. The Launch Director picked it up,

listened, grinned, and gave Neville a thumbs-up before hanging up.

"You are cleared to go," he said.

Neville nodded to the technician, who began flicking switches to start the launch process. He turned to the inspectors — government and industry men — watching to decide whether this project had a future. Their faces remained grim, understandably so after the last two disastrous launches. Neville turned back to the console, lifted the lid covering the ignition switch, and waited as a monotone voice counted down. At "one," he pressed the button.

The moment between pressing the switch and seeing the first smoke and flame was always agonizing. To Neville, it felt longer each time. Smoke billowed, red-yellow light flared, and Flying Geordie slowly lifted from the pad before gathering speed, racing up into the darkening sky. Soon, it was no more than a bright star, a comet streaking higher and higher, its tail glowing against the night.

"One minute to parachute deployment," the technician said.

Neville nodded. One more minute for things to go wrong. So far, everything had gone exactly as planned. Could it hold, and save both the program and his job?

Like a drowning man reliving his life, Neville's mind raced back through his years in rocketry. As a boy, he had launched model rockets from the beach into the North Sea, then built his own crude versions. Later, as a young man working at an armaments firm, he had listened as the chairman warned of hard times ahead—defence cutbacks after the end of the Korean war, shrinking foreign orders. It was then that the idea struck him: the company should make rockets. It had taken effort, and no small amount of cheek, for a junior engineer barely out of university to get thirty minutes with the man at the top. Astonishingly, that meeting led to another, and this time with the full Board of Directors.

The technician broke Neville's reverie. "Engine shut down." A pause, then: "Parachutes deployed."

A smile crept across Neville's face. He turned to the observers. "As you see, we're ready to move on to the next stage."

Their expressions remained stony. Neville suspected many were disappointed, especially the representatives of rival firms and their allies in government. "I hope you'll note that in your reports."

"It's not for you to decide what we report," a fussy bureaucrat snapped. Murmurs rippled through the group as they shuffled out.

When they were gone, Neville turned to the Launch Director and facility manager. "I'll take the tapes and print-outs back with me. I'll return at first light to help with recovery."

"The rocket's already on the ground," the technician said.

"Where?" Neville asked, peering out into the impene-trable dark of Spadeadam Waste.

"Exactly where it was supposed to be," the technician replied. "No wind so the descent was perfect."

Neville nodded. "I'm going to see it. I'll be back for the recordings."

He hurried from the command centre and hitched a ride in a Land Rover with two soldiers heading to the landing site.

"We're staying overnight to guard it," one soldier grinned. "How are you getting back?"

"There'll be plenty of rides," Neville said.

He was right. At the landing site, several vehicles were already there. The rocket lay among the heather, parachutes draped across the ground.

"In one piece," a soldier remarked.

Neville nodded, speechless. Years of hobby rockets launched into the sea had led to this. Despite the drizzle and gloom, his spirits soared. Whatever the observers reported to Whitehall, this launch was a triumph. Soldiers busied themselves gathering the parachutes. Rain hissed on the still-hot nozzle, sending up steam.

Neville caught a return ride to the command centre, collected the data, and drove back to the factory. Lights glowed from the rocket shed windows. He guessed who was inside.

Opening the personnel door, Neville grinned at the sight: the next rocket was already on the cradle Flying Geordie had vacated. Its skin stripped away, its frame and innards were exposed for work.

"Hey, Derek. Haven't you a home to go to?"

Derek Parker, with him from the start, looked up and grinned. "Not me. This shed is my home." It was nearly true; he spent more time there than at his parents' house.

"Everyone else gone?" Neville asked, unloading the day's results into the office safe.

"Just me and Col," Derek replied, joining him. "I hear it went well."

"Perfect," Neville said. "You should've been there."

Derek shook his head. "Too much to do getting the next one ready for me to stand around watching."

They walked toward the rocket's nose. Neville frowned. "Is this where Col was working?"

"Yeah. Why?"

"It's not like him to leave his tools like that."

Neville reached for a soldering iron left dangerously near a cable tray. The instant his fingers touched the handle, a jolt shot through him, sending him staggering back with a curse.

Derek grabbed his arm, steadying him.

"Was Col really working here?" Neville demanded, still twitching.

Derek nodded, then unplugged the iron. He scowled at the frayed cord and cracked handle. "But he wouldn't have left it like this."

"Anyone else been in here?"

"Not while I was here. I did nip across to Elsie's Café for a sandwich. Twenty minutes, tops."

"You locked up?"

Derek's look answered for him.

"Sorry—of course you did," Neville said. "Shock's made me daft."

"There was no one here when I left, no one when I came back. Col had already gone. His wife had a 'do' tonight, and he was minding the bairns."

"Someone with a key and a grudge," Neville muttered.

"But who was the target, you or me?" Derek asked.

"Anyone," Neville said grimly. "So long as someone was badly hurt, the Rocket Department would be shut down."

"Their lunacy's growing," Derek growled. "Scratching cars is one thing. This is madness."

"We need to keep quiet until the Ministry signs off on today's launch," Neville said.

"Then we need better security here. If they got in while I was gone twenty minutes, we're wide open. Guards, around the clock. That means us taking turns, because factory security's stretched thin."

Neville nodded. "I'll start tonight. I need to go through

the data anyway. You go home, rest, and come back at one or two."

"You'll be all right on your own?"

"We'll lock up tight before you go. I'll be fine."

"Need a secret knock to get back in?" Derek teased.

"Too right." Neville rapped on a cupboard to demonstrate.

With Derek gone, Neville returned to his office. Switching on the lamp, he spread out the printouts, tracing the rocket's flight. He lacked proper analysis equipment. Perhaps the Ministry would fund some now. Absorbed in the work, he hardly noticed his empty stomach until the pangs became insistent. He unplugged his kettle, filled it at the tap, and plugged it back in.

The smell of smouldering cloth around the cable didn't even register.

Chapter Four

END OF A DREAM

Once again, traffic was at a standstill on Pauline's drive to work. This time it was a fire, with fire crews blocking many roads. Through her windscreen she could see smoke rising ahead. It looked to be near her workplace, which made her uneasy. On one level, she worried production would be disrupted. On another, a more personal level, she wondered if Brenda had left her kettle plugged in overnight -- and whether she herself had failed to notice. Burning down the factory was not the managerial legacy she had in mind.

Fortunately, the office entrance was still open. Pauline parked, climbed the stairs, and from her window saw the rocket shed reduced to a smouldering shell. More disturbing, police and men in white coats were crouched around what looked very much like a body. Telling Brenda she was stepping out, Pauline hurried downstairs and crossed the yard. The stench of burned rubber, wood, and oil was foul enough, but beneath it was something worse -- burned flesh.

"Stop!" A police officer stepped forward, blocking her path.

"Who is it?" Pauline asked, gesturing toward the body.

"I'm not at liberty to say. An announcement will be made soon."

As he spoke, a pale young man was led away by a detective. Pauline recognised him as one of Neville's men from yesterday, when the rocket was wheeled out of the shed.

"Is it Neville?" she asked.

The man nodded, seeming about to speak, but the police hurried him away.

Pauline's insides went hollow. Neville, who had left only yesterday with his precious rocket, who had asked for her help in tracking down an embezzler -- was now dead. An ambulance reversed up to the cordon. That was enough; she returned to her office.

"Have they taken him away?" Brenda asked as Pauline entered.

"They're doing that now." Pauline paused, struck by Brenda's tone, as though she already knew who had died. "Do you know who it is?"

"Oh, yes. Derek was here when I arrived. He told me. He'd seen the fire first and called it in."

"What time was that?" Pauline asked.

"He said Neville had stayed to do the night shift, and Derek agreed to relieve him at two. When Derek arrived, there was already a small fire. He tried an extinguisher, but it wasn't enough, so he went to Security for help. By the time the fire service got here, it had taken hold."

Pauline frowned. "That quickly?"

Brenda nodded. "He tried again with another extinguisher, but the flames had spread. He thought Neville must have fallen asleep and left something on. He tried to reach Neville's office but couldn't."

"I can't see how that would cause such a blaze," Pauline said.

"My gran once left an iron on. Nearly burned the house down. And those sheds are full of oil and grease. Tinderboxes."

Pauline sighed. "What a dreadful thing, after yesterday's triumph."

"Bad luck," Brenda agreed. "Without Neville, there's no Rocket Department. No bright new future."

"You're not suggesting this was deliberate?"

Brenda shook her head. "No. Just bad luck."

"Did they always have a night shift?" Pauline asked, still puzzled.

"I asked that. Derek said there'd been a faulty soldering iron and they thought it best to keep watch overnight, in case someone tampered with things. But surely no one would be mad enough to burn the factory down."

Pauline said nothing, but her thoughts raced. Three years ago, she had taken Inspector Ramsay's advice and given up mysteries, save for trivial riddles. But this was different. Neville was dead—the same man who had just brought her evidence of corruption. Add to that the sabotage attempts against the rocket program… it was too much to ignore.

She dug out her old diary, found Ramsay's number, and dialled. To her relief, he answered.

"Miss Riddell, how nice to hear from you," he said warmly. "I thought you might call."

Pauline laughed. "Are you involved with this death?"

"I'm not. It's Inspector Gregson's case. But I can put you in touch."

"Please give me his number," Pauline said. "I'll also head down to the scene now. He may be there."

Ramsay read out the number and wished her good luck. She wondered if he was being sardonic.

At the cordon, she spotted a young man in a brown suit ducking under the rope. Forceful, decisive-looking.

"Inspector Gregson?" she asked.

He looked at her sharply. "Yes. Who wants to know?"

Pauline introduced herself, citing Ramsay as a character reference.

"And you have evidence?" Gregson asked.

She explained Neville's concerns.

"You think he was killed for this?"

"Not exactly," Pauline replied. "But it may bear on what happened."

"Murder for petty thievery?" Gregson raised an eyebrow.

"Perhaps it wasn't so petty."

"You think national security's involved?"

"I'm only saying, keep the possibility in mind."

Gregson nodded. "Thank you. I'll be doing a preliminary investigation. But the fire people think it was an accident -- an electrical short in a kettle. He was likely overcome by smoke before he knew it, and when the flames reached oil, the whole shed went up. The man meant to relieve him tried to save him, but too late."

"Neville was a technical whizz," Pauline protested. "He wouldn't let a fire get that far."

"Perhaps. But I'll wait for the final report. I like to keep an open mind."

"So do I," Pauline muttered, after one last look at the devastation. Then she turned back to her office, her thoughts darker than the smoke still hanging in the air.

Chapter Five

IT WAS AN ACCIDENT

The following morning, an announcement crackled over the public address system, followed by notices pinned on the bulletin boards. Neville Halliday, they said, had died in an unfortunate accident. Both the fire department and police had ruled out foul play. The message praised his foresight, his pioneering work on potential new products, and declared he would be missed by all who knew him.

Pauline frowned as she read the notice in the management corridor. Without hesitation, she phoned Inspector Ramsay.

"It's true," Ramsay told her. "The forensic people see no reason to believe it was anything other than an accident."

"Well, *I* don't believe it," Pauline retorted.

Ramsay chuckled. "I thought you might say that. But your judgment's coloured by the papers he gave you the night before. I admit, the timing is odd, but coincidences do happen."

"Why was he there at all?" Pauline demanded. "There was no night shift scheduled."

Ramsay hesitated. "You'll have to ask Derek Parker about that. Though it may only deepen your suspicions."

"Does it deepen yours?" Pauline pressed.

"If it were my case, yes," Ramsay admitted.

"And Gregson? Have you told him?"

"I have. But he has the reports from the relevant departments -- and a superior reminding him to focus on the real murder he's been assigned."

"What murder?" Pauline asked sharply.

"You must have read about it. It was in all the papers."

"Oh, yes," Pauline recalled. "The young woman they found nearby."

"She was murdered," Ramsay confirmed. "Your colleague, however, appears to have been careless. Those are the judgments we police are forced to make."

Pauline grimaced. "Then I'll investigate Neville's death myself. And when I find something, I trust you'll see it gets to the right people."

Sighing, Ramsay replied, "It's Gregson's case. He is the right people."

"You've just told me his superiors redirected him. What's the point of handing it to him?"

"That's the process, Miss Riddell. You and I must work within it," Ramsay said, with a laugh that didn't entirely mask his caution.

"But you will help?"

Ramsay paused. "If you find evidence I believe in, I'll do what I can to see it followed up. That's as far as I'll go."

Pauline thanked him and hung up. He was cautious, but she was confident that when she brought him something concrete, he would help her.

At lunch, Pauline sought out Derek. She found him staring morosely at the ruins of the rocket shed, where the charred carcass of the next rocket still lay on its cradle among the fallen roof panels.

"Have you heard what the company plans to do after this disaster?" she asked.

He nodded without looking at her.

"Will there be a chance for you to step up?"

That made him turn. "Are you mocking me? At a time like this?"

His voice shook with fury.

Pauline recoiled. "No. What do you mean?"

"You're one of the bosses now," Derek snapped. "Don't tell me you don't know."

Pauline decided this wasn't the moment to lecture him on the gulf between senior management and the executive floor. "I don't know," she said evenly. "What don't I know?"

"They've dumped us under Naval Guns, under old Morgan," Derek spat. "And he's put his lapdog, Owen, in charge."

Pauline grimaced. She saw Derek's point: the Rocket Department had been handed to its bitterest rival. "Maybe some good can come of it, if you make your case strongly enough."

"I'm not Neville. I'm no salesman," Derek snarled. "It's over. We'll be making gunpowder and cannons before long."

"Even Morgan knows naval guns are on the way out," Pauline argued. "Write a paper. Show how rockets can replace them. Catch my boss's ear. Don't give up."

But Derek only shook his head. "I've seen jobs advertised for men with rocket experience. I'll look at them."

"Think carefully, Derek," Pauline urged. "This could still be your chance. Neither Morgan nor Owen knows a thing about rockets. They need you."

He turned away, sullen, and said nothing more.

Shrugging, Pauline left him to his thoughts and headed to the management canteen. As she approached, she again saw the odd little group she'd noticed before: Violet Paisley, the giggling blonde from the typing pool; Ethel Lambton, the dour electrical engineer; and Morris Fenham, the senior manager from Purchasing. The sight puzzled her. Morris, so protective of his dignity, surely realised how such company might spark gossip—or worse, scandal

Catching Morris's eye, Pauline smiled, then joined them.

"What's good today, Morris?" she asked lightly.

"I had the steak and kidney pudding. Passable," he replied.

"Unlike my potato and leek soup," Ethel added. "Stone cold."

Violet giggled.

"You had the salad, Violet," Pauline said. "Worth trying?"

"If a girl wants to keep her figure, yes," Violet said, casting a coy glance at Morris. Her hands fluttered as she spoke, a gold chain bracelet glinting at her wrist. Pauline, no expert in jewellery, thought it looked real. That explained part of this mystery, but not Ethel's presence.

"Won't you join us, Pauline?" Ethel asked.

"You can take my seat, Miss Riddell," Violet said sweetly. "Typists only get thirty minutes."

Pauline accepted the invitation, collected a slice of currant tart with custard and tea from the serving station, and returned to find Ethel and Morris regarding her pudding with silent disapproval.

Suddenly, Ethel spoke. "Is it true Neville gave you evidence of wrongdoing in the Rocket Department?"

Pauline blinked. She hadn't expected anyone to know. "I wouldn't put it like that," she said, smiling. "He had doubts about two purchases. I was going to check, but now… well, it seems moot."

"You didn't think it serious?" Morris asked.

"I never had the chance to form an opinion," Pauline said. "Even Neville wasn't sure it was more than a mistake. He thought it might suit my new department. Said it was 'right up our street'."

Morris's expression hardened. "Suspicious invoices should have been brought to me. That's my responsibility."

Pauline ate another spoonful before replying. He was right, of course, but Neville had clearly thought Morris was part of the problem. "I expect Neville saw me and thought I should finally do some work," she said lightly. "I've felt a bit of a fraud since my department was created. Perhaps he agreed."

"Possibly," Morris said grimly. "But you should have told him to come to me."

"I would have -- if events hadn't overtaken us all."

"Perhaps you could hand me the papers after lunch. I'll have my people investigate."

Pauline smiled, masking her unease. "I'm due with the MD now, but if you drop by my office at two, I'll be back."

Morris nodded curtly. He and Ethel rose together and left with cool nods of dismissal

Pauline finished her dessert, then headed to the MD's office. Finding him out, she borrowed his assistant's phone and called Brenda, instructing her to copy the documents. Then, with thanks, she returned discreetly to her office, careful to avoid notice.

"Here are your copies," Brenda said as Pauline came in.

"Good. If Morris calls and I'm out, give him the originals -- but don't mention the copies."

Brenda looked puzzled. "There's nothing in your calendar?"

Pauline nodded. "We said two, but I want to be careful."

At precisely two o'clock, Morris appeared.

"You're back," he said brightly, with the oily smile Pauline so disliked.

"Yes. Here are the papers." She handed him the file. "Neville told me he never ordered these. They never arrived. I see why he worried, but I'm sure it's a mistake."

Morris scanned the pages. "I see this sort of thing often. One digit wrong, and an order for naval guns gets booked under artillery. Nothing more sinister."

Pauline nodded. "Likely so. Neville was too new to know the quirks."

"Poor man," Morris said smoothly. "He had so much to learn."

"You'd had dealings with him before?" Pauline asked.

"Yes. A week ago, he came with another invoice. He claimed it wasn't the Rocket Department's."

"And?"

"That was a mistake of his deputy, Derek. The parts had already arrived. The fitters were installing them when Neville stormed into my office. He hadn't been told. He was impetuous, and it embarrassed us both." Morris shook his head gravely. "I complained to my director. Very distressing."

Pauline gave him a careful smile. "Well, I'm sure this too will prove nothing. Let me know when you know."

Assuring her he would, Morris left quickly -- without his usual banter for the women in the office.

"He seemed pleased," Brenda remarked, peering in.

"For now," Pauline said.

Chapter Six

AUDITING AT LAST

Pauline spent the afternoon with her small staff, reviewing the information she'd been given by the Managing Director and assigning each of them parts of the investigation. This was the job she'd been selected to do, and she knew it had to remain her principal focus. Unfortunately, her thoughts kept straying back to the copies of the two invoices in the file on her desk, tugging at her to investigate them instead.

Finally, after an hour of questions, discussion, and planning until there was nothing left to say, Pauline brought the meeting to a close and hurried back to her desk. She had examined the two invoices carefully on the night Neville died and compared them to the papers from the MD, but now they seemed more significant than ever. Whatever the police and the company might say about Neville's death, Pauline wasn't ready to believe in coincidence.

At five o'clock, Brenda looked into Pauline's office. She was leaving for the day; did Pauline need anything before she went? Pauline assured her she didn't, wished her a good evening, and smiled with relief as the door closed behind her.

The relief was short-lived. Moments after Brenda's click-clack of heels faded along the corridor's linoleum, there came a timid knock. Pauline frowned. She hadn't heard anyone approach.

"Come in," she called, sliding open the central drawer of her desk where she kept her paperknife. When Violet slipped inside, Pauline breathed a soft sigh of relief and closed the drawer. "What is it, Violet?"

Violet lingered near the door, hesitant, as if unsure of her welcome. Pauline noticed she wore no shoes, which explained her silent arrival.

"You knew Neville, didn't you?" Violet asked.

Pauline smiled and gestured for her to sit. "A little. As a fellow employee and manager."

Violet sat down, fiddling with the gold bracelet Pauline had noticed at lunch. "He told me he'd given you some documents that would get Morris Fenham fired -- and maybe even imprisoned."

"Is that what you want?" Pauline asked.

Violet nodded, glancing nervously at the door, as though expecting Morris to appear.

"Why?" Pauline pressed. She knew why *she* disliked the man, but it hadn't driven her to want him jailed.

"I—" Violet faltered, then tried again. "Earlier in the summer, he asked me out. We went out off and on for weeks, but he grew... possessive. He bought me gifts," she lifted her arm to show the bracelet, "and grew angry if I didn't wear them. I told him I didn't want to see him again, and he would have hit me, but Neville was nearby and shouted at him."

"A white knight," Pauline said with a smile, "just where he needed to be."

Violet nodded. "I decided to end things where there were lots of people around, so Morris would have to behave. That's how frightened I was."

"But you were having lunch with him today," Pauline pointed out.

Violet shook her head. "I was with Ethel, and he joined us. I didn't know they were friends."

"I see. Odd friends, those two," Pauline mused. "They don't seem to have much in common."

"I wondered that too," Violet admitted. "But after hearing them talk, I think it's just that neither of them has any *other* friends."

Pauline laughed. "That's a good explanation. Still, it must have been difficult, having Morris sitting there."

Violet squirmed. "It wasn't quite like that."

"What was it like, then?" Pauline asked.

"After Neville saved me that day at the company picnic, he and I went out together a few times -- and then the first rocket launch failed. After that, he said he was too busy."

Pauline nodded. At the time, everyone had remarked on Neville's obsessive work habits. He was said to be living in the factory, determined to design the failure out of the second launch. "And that made you unhappy?"

Violet nodded. "I thought we were going to be a proper couple. Finally, I asked if we were going to the 'Hoppins' like we'd planned, and he laughed in my face. Said the next launch was only a week away and nothing mattered to him but that."

Pauline could understand Violet's disappointment. The 'Hoppins' was the local name for the traveling fair that camped on the edge of the city each summer and a time that everyone under thirty looked forward to. "That must have hurt," Pauline said.

"It did. Then Morris began bumping into me again. He apologised over and over, saying it was just because he loved me too much."

"So you began seeing him again?"

"For a time," Violet admitted. "It was nice -- except for the presents. I didn't want them. They were what caused the trouble last time."

Pauline nodded. "I do see. Go on."

"Well, you'll remember the second launch went well until the very end, when it veered off course. Most people were down about that, but Neville was over the moon. He said the problem wasn't so bad. He hugged and kissed me right in the office; it was embarrassing, but…"

"But enjoyable," Pauline suggested with a smile.

Violet blushed. "Yes. And when he asked me to celebrate with him, I agreed. It wasn't as if Morris and I were engaged. We'd never talked about anything serious, so I thought it would be fine."

"It wasn't?"

Violet's expression turned horrified. "He was livid. I've never seen anyone so angry. Not even my mam, and she's a nutcase."

"He didn't do anything, though?" Pauline asked.

"No, he just stormed off swearing. In a way, I was relieved. I thought Neville and I would be together, and Morris couldn't stop us."

Pauline felt a cold knot form in her stomach. Violet seemed oblivious to the dangerous rivalry forming around her. "Go on," she urged.

"Neville and I went out for a while after that, until he

buried himself in the third rocket. He was never free and barely spoke when I tried."

"Rockets were his life," Pauline said softly. "Everyone feared his obsession would break him."

Violet nodded. "I think it was the Russians who killed him."

"Why would they?" Pauline asked. "They already have a satellite. Our rockets are baby steps compared to that."

"Neville was moving quickly," Violet insisted. "He'd soon have overtaken them."

Pauline smiled faintly. "I'm sure he would. But with Neville so occupied, did Morris reappear in your life?"

"He's always around," Violet sighed. "Every day. Always ready to talk, or go out, or have fun."

Pauline nodded. "Men like Neville are unreliable in love. Their constancy is only to their true passion."

"Exactly!" Violet cried, brightening. "You understand. Nobody's perfect. You must choose what's best for yourself."

"You do indeed," Pauline agreed.

"Only, I wish he wouldn't buy such expensive presents," Violet murmured. "We'd need that money if we…"

"Has he asked you to marry him?"

Violet shook her head. "But he's going to. I know he is."

"So he hasn't been as threatening as before Neville stepped in?"

"He's been a proper gentleman," Violet said. "He explained it all, like I told you."

"And since Neville's death?" Pauline asked.

Violet beamed. "He's been so sweet. He understands how I feel. Only," she paused, "he bought me another present." Pulling back her sleeve, Violet revealed a jeweled watch.

"That looks very expensive," Pauline said. In her mind,

she recalled one of Neville's disputed invoices -- for a timer the Rocket Department had never used.

"I know. I saw one like it in town weeks ago and it cost a month's wages," Violet said, avoiding her gaze.

"And you were with Morris, and told him you liked it?" Pauline asked gently.

Violet nodded, unable to speak.

"Is this why you came to see me?"

Again, Violet nodded, then blurted out: "He came to see me at the afternoon break. Everything was fine until…"

"Until?" Pauline prompted.

"He said Neville died because he pushed himself between Morris and me. I was horrified and asked what he meant. He said he only meant Neville was pushy -- always riding roughshod over everyone. That in his drive to outdo the rest of us, he'd made a mistake and died for it."

"Clumsy men," Pauline said. "Neville in his work, and Morris with his words."

"But Neville was never clumsy," Violet whispered. "Even I know that. He was a perfectionist."

"You think Morris may have done something that caused Neville's death?"

"I don't know," Violet admitted. "But when Morris said those words—that's what I thought. And I think he saw that I thought it."

"And now you're frightened," Pauline said softly.

Violet nodded, eyes wide. "Can you have him put in prison?"

"Only if he's done something wrong," Pauline replied. "And we don't know that. But you must be careful until I've finished investigating. Go nowhere alone, and certainly not with Mr. Fenham."

"Everyone's gone home now," Violet whispered. "Can you give me a lift?"

Pauline nodded. Violet wasn't clever, and perhaps she imagined things worse than they were. But the police wouldn't act on her fears, and Pauline couldn't wait. Once again, it seemed that doughty seeker of justice Miss Riddell was needed... and quickly too.

Chapter Seven

AN ALLY

Her office phone was ringing as Pauline entered her office next morning and she snatched at it, dropping the bag full of files she'd taken home the night before onto her desk. It landed with a solid thump as she said, "Yes?"

"Good morning, Pauline," the Managing Director's voice answered.

"Good morning," Pauline responded, as she scrabbled with her free hand for a pencil or pen and paper. "What is it?"

"I have a meeting in fifteen minutes, and I want to know if you've anything to report on the project I gave you?"

Pauline would have liked to say, 'You must be joking, that was only yesterday' but sensibly replied, "It's early days, however, at least one of the files you gave me could well be the result of a simple mistake."

"Nothing jumps out at you?" he pressed her.

"As we discussed, I agree there seems to be a pattern of criminal behavior," Pauline replied, "and my staff are following up but beyond that first result, which we're still pursuing, I have nothing new."

She heard him grunt in disappointment before saying, "Pity. The meeting would have been an ideal opportunity to light some fires under peoples' backsides."

Pauline chuckled. "Sorry. By the way, I've reserved those items in the documents you gave me that pertain to the Rocket Club. There were more items than I felt was in line with the size of the department and, also, with police and safety investigations underway, I thought it best to limit the pool of people who knew about this."

'Good," he replied. "If you need anything from me, let me know."

"I thought mentioning my interest in the Rocket Club at your meeting might stir up some activity," Pauline suggested. "Like poking a stick in a stagnant pool to see what crawls out of the mud."

"An apt analogy," he told her. "If what I suspect is true and you find the evidence. I'll do that." He hung up abruptly, leaving Pauline shaking her head. She had always liked the man, and he'd done well by her, giving her that first break when she was barely established in the firm, but she had to acknowledge, his manner could sometimes be brusque.

Brenda, who'd heard the phone being reset, poked her head in and asked, "Tea?"

Pauline nodded. "Please, and then nobody comes in until I say they can." She was already making notes from the Rocket Club invoices when her morning tea arrived.

"He sounded gruff," Brenda said, as she placed the cup and saucer on the desk. "He isn't unhappy with us, is he?"

Pauline smiled and shook her head. She knew Brenda's

fear for her job all too well. "Not at all. He's just not at his best in the morning."

"Oh, good," Brenda replied. She didn't sound convinced.

"Really, Brenda. He was just in a hurry for something to take to a meeting he was attending. It's all taken care of."

Brenda smiled and relaxed a little.

"I'll be going down to Purchasing when I've finished these." Pauline gestured at the invoices she was reading. "I may not be back until lunch time, if anyone asks."

"Can I say where you are?"

"No. If you need me, phone down to Morris Fenham, and he'll find me," Pauline replied, grinning. She was sure he'd be watching her like a hawk the whole time she was in the Purchasing filing vaults.

Brenda grimaced.

"I know, but he's the manager there. You can't avoid him," Pauline reminded her.

Pauline's prediction turned out to be accurate. Morris tried at first to bar her entry into the vaults, and she had to ask him to check with his director. As the director was well aware of the MD's concerns and that Forensic Audit was investigating, Morris was soon back saying, "Very well, but if there's something you don't understand you ask me before running off to the boss with wild accusations."

Pauline assured him, he'd be the first to be asked to explain anything she didn't understand and set to work. The Rocket Club purchase orders and invoices were separately filed from the rest, which made her task straightforward. She soon had a list of questions for Morris and a bundle of orders and invoices for him to check and explain. With luck, it would prevent him from challenging Violet for the day. She turned to leave the vault and was surprised to see Bob Wallace idly observing her.

"Hello, Bob. Aren't you a little out of your way?" Pauline asked him. He was 'factory' not 'office' and it was rare to see the one in the other.

"You're looking into Neville's death," Bob replied, ignoring her question.

"I'm doing an audit on the Rocket Club, that's all," Pauline responded. "New manager and a new baseline, you know. People like to know where they stand when they take over something."

Bob nodded slowly. He clearly didn't believe her. "I heard Neville had asked you to look into the Rocket Club books too, and he weren't no new manager."

"That's probably why Luke Morgan wants this doing. He probably heard rumors," Pauline said. "Now, I must be going, and you should be too. Morris Fenham won't take kindly to uninvited guests in his vaults."

Bob shrugged. He clearly didn't find this possibility threatening. "I can help."

Pauline, who'd begun walking away stopped and turned to him. "How?"

"I did some of the ordering for the Rocket Club and some of the receiving," he replied. "Which is how I can be here, to answer your earlier question."

"And why would you help?"

Bob looked about to see they were still alone. "Fenham's a rat and he's bothering Violet. I don't like that."

"Is Violet a friend?" Pauline asked.

For the first time, Bob was unsure of himself. "She's a

work friend," he said, at last. "One I like more than most. She needs looking after, that one."

Pauline couldn't argue with that. She'd already decided Violet was a menace to herself and any single man who looked to be going places. "I see. I'm not sure your assistance would be as impartial as I need, if I'm going to make a case against Mr. Fenham."

"I'll be impartial," Bob replied. "I may be factory but I'm not a fool."

"I didn't think you were," Pauline replied, a little too quickly for her own peace of mind. His presence at the rocket roll-out and now here suggested he too was working on putting Morris Fenham behind bars and he might have started before she even knew there was a problem. "What if our investigation shows wrongdoing among one of your colleagues?"

"If we had a bad 'un among us, I'll be happy to string him up myself," Bob said. "For now, I'll be happy to get Violet out of that rat's oily paws."

Pauline nodded. "Come to my office after hours. We can talk more there." She turned and made her way back to Morris's office where, Morris, when presented with her list and the bundle exclaimed, "I can't answer all this today. These go back weeks, and I'll have to have my staff tell me what was going on at the time. I don't do the paperwork myself; you know."

"I didn't imagine you did," Pauline replied. "Perhaps your secretary would have these copied for me and then I can leave them with you."

"The best people to ask would be the Rocket Club folks," Morris grumbled, as he took the sheaf of papers out to his secretary.

As he returned, Pauline pointed out the Rocket Club

shed was gone and all their records with it. She'd have little success picking the brains of people who could be sure whatever they said couldn't be verified.

"Mebbe not," Morris conceded. "It's still worth interviewing their head men. That Derek for one."

The secretary returned with the copies before Pauline could answer, and it was only when she was sure that she had a copy of everything she'd handed over did she rise to leave. "I'll take your advice, Morris," she told him. "I believe Bob Wallace also did some of the buying over there." She was pleased to see a flicker of anger in his expression as he agreed that was so.

Pauline's mind returned to Violet's description of her relationship with Morris Fenham and shook her head in dismay. There'd been a recent movie called *An Affair to Remember*, which she'd assumed meant it was a story of blissful love. She now had another interpretation. Violet would long remember her liaison with Fenham and it was anything but blissful. There'd been another film, *Witness for the Prosecution*, which Pauline had considered going to see. Violet's story sounded much more like that.

Pauline hadn't heard from Fenham by mid-afternoon and hadn't heard anything new from her own team of investigators. She did what all leaders do; she called a meeting.

"Has anyone any good indications of wrongdoing?" Pauline asked her assembled staff sitting around the table of their department's meeting room.

There was a general lack of response, so she picked on the nearest. "John, what have you found?"

John grimaced. "The trail I'm furthest along may just be a human error. It's looking like that, anyway."

Pauline frowned. "Everything is just a 'mistake'. How is this possible? Fred, what have you to show for your efforts?"

Fred looked as uncomfortable as John had. "You aren't going to like this, but my first investigation is showing much the same thing."

Pauline shook her head in dismay. "Are we really saying the Managing Director has given us a pile of dodgy invoices and purchase orders and they're all just mistakes? He isn't going to believe people who've worked in these departments using the company's systems for decades have suddenly started making all these mistakes. 'Mistakes' is how Morris Fenham was suggesting the issues Neville left with me can be explained as well."

There was a silence before Pauline saw her youngest, newest member of staff was itching to say something. He at least would bring a fresh pair of eyes to the problem.

"Ian, what have you to show for your efforts?" Pauline demanded. Her patience was wearing thin.

"It's more of my observations," Ian replied and paused to see if the boss was willing to listen to him.

"Well, go on?"

"Two things really. The first is about the company's purchasing system. It hasn't been seriously brought up to date since its inception at the time the company began, about a hundred years ago. When I ask, I'm told 'if it was good enough for Jos Liddesdale, it's good enough for us.' But the company has expanded out of all recognition since the late 1800s and, particularly since the re-armament in the late 1930s, through the war years and into the Cold War years. The company produces vastly more of many different products and, to accommodate this, all that has been done is to add a hyphen and a number or letter to the code."

"We know all this," John interjected sharply. "It's old news. And the problems, if these invoices and orders are to be believed, only began in the past months. To be clear, since that Rocket Department began."

"Thank you, John," Pauline said, before they began squabbling. She knew the two older men were mildly jealous of the new boy with the fancy university degree. "Carry on, Ian, but get to the point."

"The point is, with so many small variations, it's easy for mistakes to be made when people are rushed," he paused for effect, "and easy for someone to claim their embezzlement is a simple mistake. It will be hard to separate real mistakes from deliberate ones."

"That's why we're employed," Fred said, sarcastically. "To identify fraud and not punish mistakes."

Ian, his expression grim but determined, continued, "My second observation is really a question, was the MD given these documents to make *him* look bad or did he give them to us to make *us* look bad?"

This final observation shocked the room, and a brief silence ensued, before Fred stated bluntly, "I still say it's the Rocket Club."

Pauline asked, "You think someone in the Rocket Department was embezzling?"

Fred looked at the others and grinned, "Or someone wanted the Rocket Club to look bad." The others chuckled as he said it.

Pauline knew instinctively that rumors must have been flying around the factory about the rivalry between Neville and Morris for Violet's affections and consequently she chose her words carefully, "A professional jealousy, you think?"

Fred laughed and shook his head. "No, though there's no doubt old Luke Morgan was furious about the department being set up outside his department. Nay, this were just a silly, single man who's never had a girlfriend in his life falling in love with a silly wench who thinks of nothing but clothes, dancing, and parties."

"You mean Morris Fenham, I presume," Pauline said in chilling tones.

Fred was not chilled. "I named no names."

"Good. Because for us to insinuate someone is embezzling company funds without any proof would be a serious matter," Pauline replied, looking at them, before continuing, "have we proof?"

They shook their heads.

"Then, gentlemen, I suggest we keep an open mind as we investigate. This many 'mistakes' is statistically impossible, so somewhere there's an embezzler or two, and it's our job to find them. Let's get to it."

The meeting broke up, leaving Pauline alone and pondering what she'd heard. It sounded like half the company believed Morris Fenham was stealing from the company to give gifts to Violet. How far up the management ranks did this knowledge go? Is this what she was supposed to prove?

And why just Morris? As she'd learned earlier, Bob Wallace seemed to be sweet on the girl as well. Was he angry at Neville's cavalier treatment of Violet? Had Bob been stealing but making it look like Morris was the culprit and using Neville to deliver the evidence to her? Neville didn't say where the evidence he handed over came from. After all, Bob bought and sold for the Rocket Department, and he'd know how to short a circuit where it might cause a fire. Every man in the country was familiar with mending electrical appliances so even an office manager like Morris could bare a wire and start that blaze.

And -- Pauline's brain was furiously racing now -- what about Ian's question regarding the boss? Had the company's recent losses in sales caused the boss to regret establishing her department? Will our inability to find anything but 'mistakes' be the excuse he needs to shut us down? Was the fire in the Rocket Department intended only to do minor damage? After all, someone baring the flex on a kettle would expect the person using it to notice the smoke and disconnect it. Was the boss regretting his Rocket Department decision and looking for a relatively harmless excuse to shut it down?

And what about Violet herself? Was she so angry with Neville's constant neglect that she'd start a fire to remove her competition? Pauline had no reason to suppose Violet didn't understand electrical cables enough to do some minor sabotage that had unfortunately turned into a tragedy, but Pauline couldn't believe Violet would have intended murder.

Finally, of course, there was the possibility of 'X', an unknown who had been stealing for reasons of their own and who, on hearing Neville had taken steps to have the financial discrepancies investigated, had tried to cover their tracks with a fire – maybe even an intended murder.

Shaking her head to clear her much too numerous thoughts, Pauline rose and left the meeting room. Maybe Morris would have dropped answers to her questions back at her office by now.

Chapter Eight

A GOOD SUSPECT

Morris hadn't provided any answers, but her boss was demanding some. Reluctantly, Pauline called him back.

"Well?" he barked.

Pauline explained what her team had uncovered.

"That's it?" he demanded. "You think we need a modern purchasing system? With what? I started the Rocket Department because we'll be out of business when the current order finishes. Unless we have a new product, no one will fund anything."

"I understand," Pauline replied. "I'm not saying everything is mistakes. Some is clearly fraudulent, but sending the thief to prison won't save the company. An improved system could stop the bleeding. We still have maintenance and ammunition contracts to carry us until a new product is ready."

"You need to act fast," he said. "And we need a new head of the Rocket Department."

Pauline took a deep breath. "Then I suggest Derek Parker, not the old guard in Naval Guns."

49

"He's too young. He can't present himself like Neville did," her boss countered.

"Then have him report to you, and you speak for him. You need a working rocket, not another plodder speaking the company line."

"I'll think about it," he said grudgingly. "But the Board wants it under Luke Morgan's department."

Pauline frowned. "You established the Rocket Department; you can't let it die. Anyway, Derek will have Ethel to keep him in line."

Ethel Lambton, Morris's lunch companion, was a long-time employee with senior experience but never promoted. Her tightly tied-back hair, severe suits, and icy expression made her intimidating.

Her boss laughed. "True enough. But having her around didn't save Neville or, if the papers you have are fraudulent, stop the embezzlement."

"Now we know the shape of the fraud," Pauline said. "I'll alert Ethel what to look for. She might catch the thief before we do."

Her boss agreed. "Who do you suspect?"

Pauline grimaced. She wasn't naming names yet. "I have a few ideas, but I'm holding my counsel."

"Be quick. This must be stopped."

After hanging up, Pauline weighed calling Inspector Ramsay but knew Ethel was the perfect ally inside the office. She only worried about Ethel's apparent connection to Fenham.

She asked Brenda to summon Ethel to the Forensic Department meeting room.

Fifteen minutes later, Ethel arrived, wearing black. Her pale skin, ice-blue eyes, and expressionless face reinforced her severe demeanor.

"You must have been shocked by Neville's death," Pauline began.

Ethel's expression didn't change. "It was likely. A young man in a hurry. Still, a shock."

Pauline explained the meeting's purpose.

"You want me to spy on colleagues?" Ethel asked coldly.

"Not at all," Pauline smiled. "Just review what's been found and watch for irregularities."

"I may not stay on as 'club secretary.' With the department moving to Naval Guns, there's no role for me."

"You got along with Neville?" Pauline asked.

Ethel shrugged imperceptibly. "I applied to lead the department, but Neville got the job. He offered and I took an advisory role."

"That was kind of him," Pauline said. She noted the bitterness in Ethel's voice.

"Always the bridesmaid, never the bride," Ethel muttered.

Pauline pressed on. "As secretary, did any orders or invoices seem odd?"

"I'm an engineer, not a clerk," Ethel replied. "How would I know?"

"Quite," Pauline said. "Let me show you what we found."

Ethel scanned the documents. "No wonder there are mistakes. To anyone but a pedant, they're the same."

Pauline smiled. "We'll advise a new system in our report."

"They both have Neville's name," Ethel observed. "Why didn't he notice?"

"He did. He brought these papers to me the night before he died."

"Lucky for someone," Ethel replied, her tone carrying a trace of amusement.

"Unlucky for Neville, however," Pauline countered.

Ethel returned her gaze without flinching.

The meeting ended. Ethel promised to watch for irregularities and left. Pauline felt uneasy about her cold, emotionless manner. Staff would never flourish under Ethel.

Pauline examined key orders and invoices. One signature eluded identification.

"Brenda, get Bob Wallace on the phone," she called.

Bob answered promptly. "You have a question?"

"Who should I talk to about goods received at the Rocket Club loading bay?"

"You need Terry Nolan and Chris MacDonald," Bob replied.

Pauline studied the scrawl, but it could be neither.

"Could we meet?" she asked.

"I'll drop by," Bob said, warning about his new boss's watchfulness.

Thirty minutes later, Bob arrived. Together, they matched the signatures, leaving one illegible scrawl unidentified.

"I'll ask Purchasing to provide all documents," Bob advised.

Pauline agreed, noting that by the time orders reached the top, Morris might have removed incriminating items.

She arranged to speak with the loading dock men at a neutral pub after work.

Outside the *Seven Stars*, Pauline looked at the sky, searching for Pegasus and the elusive Sputnik. Shivering, she whispered to herself, "Feet on the ground, eyes peeled, Pauline, or you won't need to worry about Russians anymore."

Chapter Nine

MORE EVIDENCE

Bob and Terry were sitting in the Snug, a smaller, more private room at the *Seven Stars* pub, when Pauline arrived. Bob introduced her, and Terry nodded -- a typical Tyneside working-man greeting.

"Chris couldn't be here," Bob explained as Pauline sat.

She understood perfectly, the men distrusted scabs and snitches.

Pauline drew out the documents with the indecipherable signature and handed them to Terry. "Do you know whose handwriting this is?"

Terry shook his head. "And I don't remember any of these parts coming into our bay."

Bob added, "The company uses these parts and suppliers, but not to my knowledge the Rocket Club."

"Nor mine either," Terry replied. "These have the wrong department number."

"It's a common mistake," Pauline said.

"It happens," Terry agreed, "but not a lot. We all know

our jobs. Usually it's a new hire or a student, something like that."

Pauline nodded. "There wouldn't have been students working in the plant when this order was typed. Any new people recently?"

Terry shrugged. "I wouldn't know. Personnel can tell you."

Bob interjected, "Might explain the unidentifiable signature."

Pauline smiled. "It takes years to develop a scrawl like that, but you may be right. I'll speak to Personnel in the morning."

Terry nodded. "We haven't hired since we didn't get that Indian contract."

Pauline noted the possibility anyway; someone retiring could bring a replacement. "Did anything strike you as odd in those days leading up to the fire?"

Terry paused mid-pint. "We had something arrive that had nothing to do with us. The purchase order said it was, but Neville rejected it."

"What was it?" Pauline asked, excitement rising.

"Radio parts," Terry replied, "not for industrial use, more like something for home."

"Maybe someone ordered the wrong part?" Bob offered.

"Could be," Pauline agreed. "Anything else?"

"Two items should have arrived but didn't," Terry continued. "Neville was to chase them up. I don't know if he did."

Pauline understood why Neville was suspicious. One missing item was described as a chain, but it weighed almost nothing.

"That was about a week before the fire," Terry added.

"Neville took the documents to investigate, so I can't confirm more."

Pauline thought of the gold chain bracelet Violet wore. Could Morris Fenham's small "mistakes" have escalated to a bigger crime, driven by love or desperation? She would need the police's view.

Inspector Ramsay, predictably, was deflating.

"Miss Riddell," he said, "you make a good case for a murderer, but the fire and forensic reports show no evidence Neville Halliday was deliberately killed."

"That only means the fire destroyed evidence," Pauline argued. "Would you like to see the evidence we've gathered that suggests foul play? Even if it doesn't prove murder?"

"This is Inspector Gregson's case," Ramsay said. "He should see your documents and take your statement."

"If he believes there's no murder, he won't be interested."

"Then we'll consider what's to be done afterward. For now, let Gregson wash his hands of it. Your papers suggest possible embezzlement, which is a criminal case only if your employer pursues it."

True. Companies preferred quiet solutions: a repayment, a quiet dismissal, no public fuss.

Pauline spent the evening organizing her evidence, reflecting on her perceived rustiness. "I should have something real to show by now," she muttered, "though it was only three years ago I was sharpest."

"I'll interview Derek Parker properly in the morning," she added, turning off the bedside lamp.

Finding Derek, the next morning took effort, had Brenda phoning around what seemed like half the company offices. When she eventually tracked him down and passed Derek on to Pauline's phone, she said, "I don't think he's happy, be careful."

Pauline greeted Derek with a cheery "good morning", hoping to lighten his mood.

"If you say so," he growled in response.

"Not in your part of the world, obviously," Pauline retorted.

"I have a new office in Naval Guns," he explained, quietly. "It was a broom closet until yesterday. It doesn't even have a window."

"I assume it's because with the rocket building gone, we're short of office space," Pauline offered neutrally.

"We can assume that, of course," he replied. "What is it you wanted anyway. I'm sure you didn't phone to ask how I was."

"I want to talk about the Rocket Club's final days, particularly purchase orders and invoices."

Derek laughed. "Oh, that. Does it matter now?"

"It might explain what happened," Pauline replied.

He considered. "I can't just walk out; I'm watched."

"Surely, you're imagining things," Pauline replied. "This is England, not the Soviet Union."

"And this is office politics, not a social club," Derek retorted. "We can meet at lunchtime, away from the factory or not at all."

"Where?"

"At the Haymarket bus stop, the Whitley Bay platform. Ten past twelve. Don't be late."

Pauline drove there cautiously, stopping only when she saw him.

Derek jumped into the car. "You weren't followed?"

Pauline shook her head, smiling. "I'm sure none of this is necessary."

"You think Neville was murdered, but I'm paranoid?" Derek scoffed.

"Maybe Neville was killed for reasons beyond the Rocket Club," Pauline replied.

He shook his head. "If it's jealousy over Violet, I can relax."

"I don't really know Neville was murdered," Pauline countered.

"It was the night of a launch," Derek said, ignoring her objection. "Anyone who knew us would know who was there."

Pauline made a mental note of his statement. "That's the sort of thing I want to know. Who, what, why, where, when, all the threads of everyday life in the Rocket Club and particularly in those final days."

"Final days is right," Derek responded. "It won't be resurrected, believe me."

"Even old Luke Morgan must know it's a choice between your rockets and the dole," Pauline protested. "They need you and your expertise; you must stand up right now. This is your chance to show what you're made of."

Derek nodded. "You're right. I'm just so angry at what's happened and what's happening, I can barely think at all, let alone straight. What went on in those last days? Let me see?"

He lapsed into silence while Pauline slowly drove out of the bus terminal and back toward the factory. When she'd parked in a side street and he still hadn't spoken, she asked, "Well?"

Derek came out of his reverie, saying, "You must understand we were all focused on the coming launch. The previous one hadn't gone well, and we were terrified this one would do just as badly in front of observers from the Ministry of Defence and other industry leaders who were also competitors."

"I do understand," Pauline replied. "But Neville had time to see a problem and bring it to me, so it wasn't all about the launch."

"Neville showed me those orders and invoices about two days before," Derek continued. "I told him about the problem the loading dock men had raised with me. But I rarely dealt with paperwork of that sort. It was more Ethel and Bob's territory than mine."

"I've spoken to both of them, and they didn't mention any suspicious activity," Pauline interjected.

"Then those two documents, and the dock men's issues were likely just mistakes," Derek replied.

"Neville didn't think so."

Derek growled, "We were worried out of our minds by the problems with the guidance system and these irritants coming on top of that just drove him to overreact." His expression now was dark, angry.

"Perhaps you're right," Pauline said, smiling. "Only, there are many more such documents in the system, which suggests there's a problem somewhere."

"Not in the Rocket Department," Derek snapped, and then paused and frowned, his expression lightened.

"No, wait. I've just remembered something. It wasn't recent but it was wrong."

Heartened, Pauline asked, "What was it? When was it?"

"Back in the spring," Derek replied. "I ordered a radio part for the guidance system and the purchase order went off. The part arrived on time."

Pauline laughed. "Arriving on time was wrong?"

Derek shook his head and frowned again at her levity. "Don't be daft. My point is everything to do with our order was normal and right, but…" he paused for effect, "a little while later, I happened to see my order and invoice on Morris Fenham's desk. I was talking to him for some reason. And I saw that another part had been added to my order."

"What did he say?"

"He said it was for another department and had been added to cut down on paperwork," Derek replied. "I asked if we hadn't paid for both parts, and he assured me we hadn't. It was often done by Purchasing in these cases and wasn't something I needed bother about."

"You were happy with his explanation?" Pauline asked.

"Not entirely, but I'm not in Purchasing and provided we hadn't paid for the added part, I couldn't see any reason to object," Derek replied, but his expression was puzzled.

"But?" Pauline probed.

Derek responded, "My problem with what I saw was the part being ordered isn't something an industrial company would use, as a rule. It was more like something an amateur radio enthusiast would order."

"Is Morris Fenham an amateur radio enthusiast?" Pauline asked.

"I've no idea," Derek said, "and it may not have been him who added it. He's the Manager of Purchasing, I doubt he does a lot of the actual work."

Pauline nodded. It was true. Someone in the department could be the culprit. After all, it was unlikely Morris would know what any of the items being purchased were. A thought occurred, "You said this was back in the spring. Do you remember exactly when?" Could this tie into Morris's earlier courtship of Violet?

Derek couldn't remember and with little else left to discuss, Pauline dropped him far away from the factory to be sure he was unobserved by watchers, though she still felt his paranoia was extreme. Did his fear mean he knew something he wasn't saying?

Driving back to the factory, she decided she needed to know more about Violet and Morris Fenham. Maybe Bob Wallace could shed light on that. He may be somewhat too old for love, in his forties if he was a day, but he certainly felt something for Violet. A fatherly interest, maybe. Could there be a motive there?

Chapter Ten

ANOTHER SUITOR FOR VIOLET?

Later that afternoon, Brenda brought Bob to Pauline's office.

When Brenda closed the door behind herself and Bob was seated, Pauline asked quietly, "Tell me all you know about Morris Fenham and Violet."

"You should ask *them*," Bob replied. "I don't like gossip or informing on others."

Pauline smiled. "I'm not asking for their secrets, only what you know about their relationship. They've both told me what they wanted me to know, but a neutral observer's view would help as well."

Bob nodded, considering whether this was enough to allay his principles. "I can only tell you what I observed," he began. "Not what I thought."

"That's all I need," Pauline replied. "I'm getting a very definite picture of what developed here, and I want to be sure I'm not assuming too much."

Bob frowned thoughtfully. "Where to start. That's the problem," he said, before continuing, "To me, it began about a year ago, when I noticed Morris Fenham sniffing around Violet like a sick puppy. She wouldn't have anything to do with him, of course. He's nearly old enough to be her father, and she had a group of friends her own age, boys and girls."

"When you say 'sniffing,' he wasn't being obnoxious or anything?" Pauline asked.

Bob laughed. "No, just watching her with longing eyes, sitting as close as he could in the cafeteria, trying to engage her in conversation if they met in a corridor -- and they did seem to meet frequently away from their desks."

"Do you think Violet was encouraging him?" Pauline interjected.

Bob shook his head. "Nay. It was just that his office has a window into the corridor, and she had to pass that way whenever she had errands to run."

"I see," Pauline replied, nodding. "So Morris was clearly 'courting' Violet late last year. I had the impression it all began earlier this year."

"You're right there," Bob told her. "It began earlier this year, but he was circling as late as last year."

"Like a vulture," Pauline said with a chuckle.

Bob nodded. "Then she fell out with her boyfriend of the time at Christmas, and Morris was there with a shoulder to cry on."

"A father figure," Pauline surmised, "as you said."

Bob agreed, then continued, "I was becoming anxious when she was suddenly Neville's girlfriend. I don't know how that happened. I'd never seen Neville with a girl before. Rockets were his only true love. He lived and breathed them."

"Reminds me of those new songs, *Bye Bye Love* and *Singing the Blues*," Pauline said, chuckling. "Writers sometimes capture the times better than they know. Violet's dates with Neville must have been…" she paused, searching for an apt word, "…erm, 'interesting' for Violet."

Bob laughed. "Aye. She'd learn a lot about rocketry and little about life with Neville as her boyfriend, that's for sure. Still, I thought it better for both of them. Healthier, like."

"Is Violet a relation of yours?" Pauline asked, her curiosity getting the better of her discretion.

Bob flushed and looked at his hands. "No," he said. He seemed about to stop there before realizing that would give him away. "Her family and I are neighbors. I've known Violet since she was a child. She's a silly girl in many ways but always means well. She loves everyone and hurts no one. Despite her mini-skirts and other fashionable flirtatiousness, she's not a promiscuous girl at all. Far from it."

Pauline nodded. "You don't want to see her hurt?"

"I don't," Bob replied. "And that's where I saw her heading with Morris. I don't mean he's a violent man, only that he's a jealous one, and he'd crush the life out of her. Neville, on the other hand, was so disengaged she could dance naked in the Haymarket bus terminal, and he'd never notice."

"Not good either then," Pauline responded.

Bob nodded. "Not good, but not as bad. And Neville might have grown up with Violet around. Her liveliness may have infected him in time, especially if the rockets became successful and he wasn't so anxious about them. Or, conversely, if they'd flopped and he'd been returned to being a regular everyman engineer."

"Violet told me she'd given up on Neville," Pauline said, returning to her inquiries.

"She did," Bob said. "The rockets were too strong a pull for Neville, and I could see she felt neglected. Morris, of course, was still hovering and once again he was there to help her through her dismals."

"*You* didn't think of helping?" Pauline asked. "She'd known you since she was a girl. She might have welcomed your support."

Bob laughed. "I was twenty when she was born. I've watched her grow and, yes, played with her when she was a girl, it's true. But when she became a young woman, she saw me as an old man."

"You're the same age as Morris, and she keeps dating him," Pauline pointed out.

Bob grinned. "Morris dresses as if he's still in his twenties, dyes his hair more than Violet does, and can talk your ears off about the latest hits. Peter Pan has nothing on him."

"What dates would you put on this string of events?" Pauline asked, not commenting on Bob's sarcastic description of Morris, though she wished Bob would make a similar effort to join in the modern world. *She* didn't, and she knew why. She didn't want to encourage anyone to think of taking the place of her now long-dead fiancé, Stephen. But Bob had a crush on Violet, and he should wake up. If Violet wanted someone to share her interests, why let it be Morris?

"When I first noticed Morris's interest," Bob replied, "last November, I'd say. Then January, when he and Violet began seeing each other." He paused, getting the times straight in his mind. "Then March, when I first saw Violet and Neville together. They were together over Easter time, I remember."

This fitted very well with the dates on the earliest invoices Pauline had on her desk, and her excitement was rising.

"Violet said that when that rocket launch went wrong, Neville told her he was too busy to see her anymore," Pauline said. "Is that what you saw?"

Bob nodded. "Yes, that's right. And she and Morris were soon together again."

"Violet mentioned expensive gifts. Did you see that?"

Bob shrugged. "What man doesn't buy his girlfriend gifts? And Morris has nothing else to spend his money on." Before Pauline could reply, he continued, "Except his ham radio hobby, and I think he already has everything there."

"He's an amateur radio hobbyist," Pauline said, nodding. "I should've guessed."

Bob laughed. "He's been doing it for years. When we were younger, he drove us all mad rabbiting on about talking to people in Tokyo and other places."

Pauline felt she had what she needed and asked, "Anything more you can remember?"

Bob's expression became one of concentration. "Just one thing. There was a week or so when Violet and Neville seemed to be together again. That would be two weeks ago, maybe. I didn't know they were -- it just looked like that to me. And Morris was angry, which confirmed it in my mind."

Pauline thanked him and, when Bob was gone, phoned Inspector Ramsay, who reminded her this was Inspector Gregson's case.

"And is the case still going?" Pauline demanded.

Ramsay laughed. "It's still open, but we've moved on to other things."

"Have you spoken to Inspector Gregson, as you said you would?" Pauline continued. "Last time we spoke, you told me there was no evidence of murder, so it isn't likely the case is continuing in any meaningful sense, is it?"

"I've spoken to him," Ramsay replied, "and learned he's been re-assigned to yet another earlier case. You probably heard of the smuggling haul we stopped recently."

Pauline agreed she had and asked how that was more important than a man's death.

"If he'd been murdered," Ramsay replied, "it wouldn't be. Only, we have nothing to say it wasn't a tragic accident. Anyway, it's being investigated by the fire department as such, so we're back to fighting crime."

"Then I have a crime for you," Pauline retorted. "Embezzlement and murder."

"Do you have evidence?" Ramsay asked.

"I have more evidence than I had last time we spoke," Pauline replied, her tone more sober now. Shouting at her friend wouldn't win his assistance, she was sure of that. "Only it isn't conclusive. I'd like your help to make it so."

"I can't just investigate things for pleasure, Miss Riddell," Ramsay replied. "If your company wishes to involve the police in this embezzlement you're investigating, they have to ask for it."

Pauline was aware the company wouldn't ask for police help over an employee stealing money for trinkets and replied, "They will when we prove it led to murder."

"What kind of help are you after?" Ramsay asked.

"Any criminal record that the participants in the drama might have."

"I can't let you see police files," Ramsay replied. "However, I could point to times and places that you might find in the newspapers. This is where your old friend Poppy was so useful."

Pauline agreed it was. Poppy had become a newspaper reporter and, on the back of Pauline's first two cases, had been offered a job in the big city. A national newspaper in

London had offered her a place, and she was gone. As she and Pauline had fallen out before she left, Pauline hadn't kept in touch. It had been some time since she'd even thought of her old friend, and lately Pauline had begun to feel guilty about that. Poppy hadn't contacted her either, which made Pauline feel better, but not quite comfortable.

"Have you heard from her lately?" Ramsay asked.

"No," Pauline replied. "I imagine she's too busy. I certainly have been."

"Give me the names," Ramsay said. "I'll see what I can do."

Pauline listed the names she was interested in and was surprised when Ramsay stopped her at Ethel Lambton.

"I know her," he said. "Have done for some years. I doubt she has a criminal record."

"Why?" Pauline asked. She'd been sure there would be something nasty hiding behind that sour exterior.

Ramsay said, "She lives with her parents, always has done, and looks after them now they're retired. They're strict chapelgoers. The same chapel we went to when my family was alive. She's always first to volunteer to do good works. You won't find a kinder, milder woman in the county."

Remembering Ethel's severe, sour expression, Pauline snorted in an unladylike way she would have condemned in anyone else. "You only have to look at her to know she's none of those things, Inspector."

"Don't judge a book by its cover; isn't that how the saying goes?" Ramsay asked.

"I still want you to look at her background, Inspector," Pauline reiterated.

Ramsay chuckled. "I will, but I'm telling you what everyone here in our neighborhood will tell you. You must realize, when people grow up in the chapel, they often view the world and find it, and us, wanting."

"Still…" Pauline began, only to be cut off.

"And, as you should know, she's a highly regarded engineer at that company where you work. She has patents and awards to prove it."

Pauline had forgotten this, but quickly recovered, saying, "I'm sure there've been crooked patent holders before now."

Ramsay laughed. "I'm not convincing you, am I? Never mind. If you choose to believe that people who are sour-faced are natural criminals, I can't stop you. I hope, when I report her unblemished record, you'll acknowledge that someone being unattractive doesn't mean they would harm anyone."

"I know, Inspector," Pauline agreed. "I just don't want to miss anyone and find later they were the one. When can you give me your findings?"

"Tomorrow night, I should have something, if there's anything to find—which I doubt," Ramsay replied. "Now let me get on with my work, and you should get back to yours."

Confident he'd do as she asked, Pauline said goodbye. Ramsay's jibe about her doing her work touched a nerve, and she opened the file of papers and began examining the few remaining ones she hadn't finished. She was engrossed in them when her desk phone rang. She picked it up and said, "Yes?"

"It's the MD," Brenda told her. "Should I put him through?"

Pauline laughed. "You better had; in case he comes looking for me in person."

"Pauline," her boss said when they were connected. "What have you got for me?"

Pauline briefly explained the evidence she had and suggested it likely pointed to embezzlement.

"How much?"

Pauline would have liked to say thousands of pounds, but had to admit it was likely less than a hundred -- unless more turned up.

"Any idea who?" her boss asked.

"Yes, but it's too early to be certain," Pauline replied. "If someone is to be fired, I'd like to be sure it's the right one."

"How long before you are sure?"

"I'm meeting my people in the morning to correlate everything we have," Pauline told him. "I expect that will finally decide the matter."

"Meet them today. Tonight," her boss replied. "I want an answer before a meeting I'm attending first thing tomorrow."

"What will you recommend doing?" Pauline asked.

"I'll recommend bringing in the police," he replied. "I know it's harsh, but the company is struggling. We need to wake people up. The old days where we looked the other way when people took trifles must end. It's a fight for our lives, and every penny the company has must be spent wisely on the business."

When he rang off, Pauline had Brenda bring her staff together. She outlined her conversation with the Managing Director, then asked, "Does anyone have sufficient confidence in what they've seen to say who?"

Ian nodded. "I've finished my part, and I'm confident Morris Fenham's the man."

This bold assertion galvanised the others into agreement, though Pauline was sure that if she'd asked one of them first, they wouldn't have said so. Unlike Ian, who was relatively new, they'd known Morris for years and their code wouldn't have allowed them to name him.

"I'm afraid my investigations point to Morris Fenham too," Pauline said. "Have your papers ready to show the story -- and lock them safely away. I suspect we'll have the police here by noon tomorrow."

Taking this as dismissal, her staff nodded and left the room in silence. She understood that. Her own insides felt like water at what would happen next, and their role in it. Morris wasn't an unpopular man, and many would take his part.

Chapter Eleven

RAMSAY JOINS THE CASE

It was afternoon before the police arrived in the person of Inspector Ramsay, who gave Pauline a meaningful glance as he was led into the Managing Director's office for a briefing. Pauline, who had been laying out the evidence to the MD and the other Directors when the police appeared, found she wasn't considered important enough for this initial meeting and reluctantly returned to her office to wait.

She didn't have long to wait. The MD, Inspector Ramsay, and a constable entered her office unannounced, Brenda being absent from "her guard post," as she called her desk. Ramsay looked much as she remembered him, though the hair at his temples was a little grayer.

The MD introduced Ramsay to Pauline formally, though it was clear Ramsay had briefed him during their walk down the corridor.

"I do know Inspector Ramsay," Pauline said, shaking his hand. "We were a sleuthing team on a number of murders a few years ago."

Before Pauline could say more, the MD added, "Inspector Ramsay is here about the thefts, Pauline. Neville's death isn't part of that."

Pauline smiled. "I understand."

"Then I'll leave you to explain your findings to the Inspector," the MD told them. "I've some people I need to alert."

When he'd gone, Ramsay asked, "Are you sure of this, Miss Riddell? These signatures could be anybody's."

Pauline handed him a sheaf of papers, all signed by Morris. "Your handwriting people will see the similarity, I'm sure."

Ramsay nodded. "It's an awful scrawl, but I agree. They're the same."

"Shouldn't your financial experts be here as well?" Pauline asked.

Ramsay laughed. "They are here. Only the Directors wanted so much from them that I slipped away. They'll be with us soon enough."

"The problem is the amount, I imagine," Pauline replied. "The MD is very good at getting his way, but I can't believe the others will be happy with so much public exposure over such a small sum. Any one of the warehouse workers probably takes as much."

"Your boss says management must be held to a higher standard," Ramsay replied. Then, with a grin, he added, "Maybe some of *them* have guilty consciences too."

"As a policeman," Pauline said seriously, "you should be careful about casting aspersions on innocent people."

"You're quite right, Miss Riddell," Ramsay replied, not in the least put out by her rebuke. "Only, when a company starts a new department wholly directed at auditing its books..." He left the thought unfinished as he continued scanning the documents she'd provided. After a moment, he went on, "I assume this Fenham fellow is the one you believe started the fire that killed the rocket man?"

Pauline nodded. "They were both involved with the same young woman."

Ramsay smiled. "You said. Though I don't have the impression the rocket man was all that interested."

"He was so absorbed in his rockets, he barely noticed anyone, let alone poor Violet. The problem was, Violet seemed to like him better than she liked Fenham."

"From these letters," Ramsay observed, "Fenham seems a pompous little man. And if he is the embezzler, his takings are small. Do you really think him the type to leap from petty theft to arson and murder?"

Pauline frowned. She had considered this too. "Love does strange things to people, so I'm told. And maybe he thought what he was doing was a small act of sabotage, just enough to have Neville demoted for carelessness. He may not have thought it through, or understood the risk of lighting a fire in a building full of oil and rocket fuel."

"And this is the one Halliday brought to you?" Ramsay asked, holding up an invoice.

Pauline nodded. "He refused to sign off. Said he'd never ordered that part and never would -- it was completely wrong."

"He'd taken it to Purchasing before bringing it to you?" Ramsay asked.

"He had, and they told him it was his department number and his signature on the Purchase Order," Pauline said, pointing to the other sheet Ramsay held, "and that he had to sign off on it."

"And you think that if he hadn't taken his suspicions to Purchasing, he might still be alive?" Ramsay asked.

Before Pauline could reply, two men in suits were shown in by Brenda.

"Our financial experts," Ramsay said, introducing them to Pauline. "I'll let them ask the questions now."

With three policemen seated across from her, Pauline found the next fifteen minutes nerve-wracking. Unlike Ramsay, the financial men didn't frame their questions politely. It was an interrogation, and she knew it.

After all the documents had been discussed, the older of the two suddenly smiled -- a cold accountant's smile -- and said, "You must understand we can't assume your motives here are pure, Miss Riddell. We must treat everything we see and read with suspicion."

Pauline nodded and gave them a wry smile. The thought that they might suspect her of being the culprit, or at least a biased prosecutor, hadn't occurred to her, and the realisation stung. "Of course you must investigate with an open mind."

They took their leave, Ramsay escorting them out. Left alone, Pauline sat frantically trying to remember whether she had ever said or done anything that Fenham's defence lawyer might twist to suggest she'd framed him. She was still turning this over when Ramsay returned.

"Well?" Pauline asked.

"We're going now, and we're taking Morris Fenham with us," Ramsay replied. "Maybe when he sees the evidence, and how small the charge will be, he'll confess and throw himself on the mercy of the court."

"He won't if he had anything to do with that fire," Pauline replied. "That's what will convince me he's a murderer."

Ramsay nodded. "I should warn you; our financial fellows are very put out about this case. They're used to major crimes and don't like soiling their hands on this kind of thing. It offends their dignity."

"I got the impression they weren't pleased about something," Pauline said, laughing. "I thought it was me."

"Your boss will come to regret his decision, I fear," Ramsay said. "They want to go through the company's books. If there was this fraud at a lower level, what might they find elsewhere?"

"Their dignity demands it," Pauline replied. "I fear I might be out of a job too, if the boss takes the blame for anything they find. It was on his watch, after all."

Ramsay nodded. "Sadly, once these things start, you never know where they end. I'll keep you informed about your friend Fenham." He closed the door, leaving Pauline once again nervously anticipating her future.

Brenda entered Pauline's office only when she was sure Ramsay wasn't coming back. "He said they'd taken Morris Fenham. Is that true?"

"Very likely," Pauline replied. "But we should wait for an announcement before telling anyone."

"Everyone in the offices will know," Brenda exclaimed. "And what does this mean for us?"

"Nothing will change for us," Pauline said, though she was tempted to cross her fingers like children do when they tell a lie. "In fact, we might have more work assisting the police with their enquiries."

"Violet will be happy Morris has gone," Brenda said. "He's been bothering her for days now."

"Nothing serious, I hope?" Pauline asked, alarmed.

Brenda shook her head. "No, just stupid men's stuff.

75

He's potty about her, he really is. And at his age, it's embarrassing for her."

Pauline laughed. "Embarrassing is fine. I was worried he might have become aggressive."

Brenda gave her a puzzled look. "Morris? Aggressive?"

"She told me he was sometimes angry with her," Pauline said. "I thought I might have misjudged him."

Brenda snorted. "If she doesn't want him angry, she should stop playing fast and loose with him. And now Neville is gone, maybe she will."

"You think she should consider Morris for a husband?" Pauline asked, bewildered. She couldn't imagine any woman considering Morris a catch.

"For all her good looks and appealing ways," Brenda retorted, "she's nought but a silly child. Morris might provide the maturity she needs -- when he grows out of his infatuation."

"He's a bit silly himself," Pauline said.

Brenda shook her head. "It's only since he fell for her. Up until last winter, he was a sensible enough man. He's no catch, I'll grant you, but he has a good job, a home, and standing in the community. Not every man needs to be Cary Grant."

"I suppose," Pauline replied, thinking this was a conversation that needed to end before she started feeling guilty about her role in Fenham's fall. "It's a police matter now, and I'm sure if Mr. Fenham is innocent, he'll be released."

She didn't have long to wait. The MD called a meeting of executives and senior managers in the boardroom, and Pauline heard the message to be passed on to staff. It was simple: there was evidence of wrongdoing in the company's Purchasing process. As head of Purchasing, Morris Fenham was being interviewed by the police. No one should infer he was responsible until the police confirmed it.

Pauline shared this with her staff, who listened in silence. With no questions forthcoming, she dismissed them and advised them to say nothing. Many in the company would consider everyone in that room guilty of informing on a co-worker -- and many would think that deserved a violent response.

When they had gone, Pauline had Brenda bring Violet to her office to gauge her feelings.

"At least you aren't in any danger now he's in custody," Pauline told her.

Violet, however, seemed unimpressed. "Him? He's a drip."

"You were frightened when we spoke the other day," Pauline said.

"I needn't have been," Violet said. "He's hardly a man at all."

"You thought he'd be angry?"

"If he had real feelings, he would have been. Wouldn't he?" Violet asked.

As the question seemed genuine, Pauline suggested that a man of Morris Fenham's age was probably past the intensity that came with being young and in love.

Violet considered this. "Then maybe it's all right," she said at last. "I do feel sorry for him, though. If he did cause the fire, you can be sure he never meant to hurt anyone."

Seeing that office solidarity was as strong as that of the workers -- and that sympathy had now shifted from Neville to Morris -- Pauline agreed this might be so. Violet left, saying how much she hoped it would all turn out for the best. Pauline was left to wonder whether Morris Fenham really was as docile as everyone now claimed. It was a hard question: nobody became a manager without some degree of strength in their character, and yet…

Pauline drove home that evening still mulling over the case before her. And it was a case — a murder case, she was sure. As she locked her car doors, she gazed up at the dark sky and muttered, "Who do I phone in Moscow to get the film from Sputnik's camera, if it has one, for that night?"

Chapter Twelve

GOOD SUSPECT EXONERATED

The following morning, Pauline had only just arrived in her office when Brenda told her Morris Fenham was waiting to see her. Surprised, Pauline hung up her coat and hat before saying, "Show him in."

Morris walked into the office in triumph -- or that was how she saw it. There was a spring in his step she had never noticed before.

"Good morning," he said, beaming -- until Brenda closed the door. Then, instantly, his expression turned cold and menacing.

If Pauline had been shocked at his arrival, this sudden change chilled her even more. It was like a light switch: on, then off.

"Good morning, Morris," Pauline said, gesturing to a guest chair. "What can I do for you?"

"You can stop manufacturing lies about me, for a start," he snarled.

Despite his tone, Pauline was too fascinated by the transformation -- from swaggering confidence to simmering fury.

The effect was made even stranger by his appearance: dressed like a teenage Mod, in a ruffled shirt, a sharp Italian suit, and a feminine hairstyle. Whoever had told her about his hair was right, it was dyed a bright, golden blond.

"I've simply handed over documents to the police," Pauline said at last. "If from that you deduced I told them you forged them, you're mistaken."

"I recognized the letters you used to match the signatures," he shot back. "They were official memos to you -- not meant to set me up as a thief. Who made you do it? The MD? My director?" His voice rose to a near-shout.

Pauline's first thought was Violet. She must find a way to persuade Violet to distance herself from this man.

"I recognized the signatures on the invoices from the memos I received from you," Pauline replied, keeping her tone neutral. "How could I not? If you didn't sign the fraudulent orders, you have nothing to worry about."

He laughed. "I have nothing to worry about at all. I denied signing them, and their handwriting expert could only say they looked similar. I don't know why you set them on me, but I'm telling you to quit. Find another victim, you bitter bitch. This is why no one likes you. Sucking up to the boss only takes you so far. Remember that."

He rose and strode out of the office.

"At least Violet would have been impressed," Pauline muttered. "He finally found his anger, and someone to vent it on." The meeting, however, had settled the argument in her mind. His thin veneer of soft charm was for Violet alone, concealing a nasty streak a mile wide.

Brenda poked her head around the door. "Everything all right?"

Pauline nodded. "Did you hear any of the conversation?"

"No, but I heard the tone," Brenda replied. "I'm going to warn Violet. She needs to know."

"I was thinking the same," Pauline agreed. "It will come better from you."

Brenda slipped away quickly, hurrying down the corridor. Pauline doubted Violet would react as Brenda hoped, but her secretary's absence gave her an opportunity. She called the Managing Director and was put on hold until he finished another call.

When he came on, he said, "I can guess why you're phoning."

"Probably," Pauline replied. "Is it wise to have Fenham back in the building?"

"Wise or not, we've no grounds for barring him," the MD replied. "He was interviewed and released, like any other honest citizen."

As she had expected, Pauline found no argument strong enough to contradict him. Her recent encounter with Fenham would sound like sour grapes. Instead, she asked: "My principal question is -- are we to continue investigating the purchasing system, or have the police financial investigators put us out of business?"

"They're looking at the bigger picture," her boss replied. "For now, continue. I'll let you know if we're ordered to stop."

With that assurance, Pauline passed on the news to her staff. They weren't pleased.

"I've already had threats," Fred, the oldest of them, said. "To carry on today, with Fenham strutting around, will be like waving a red rag at a bull."

"Then start quietly in the vault," Pauline advised. "This may have been going on months, even years."

She left them to decide how to proceed without drawing Fenham's attention.

Back in her office, she found Inspector Ramsay with an anxious Brenda standing guard.

Pauline grinned. "Thank you, Brenda. Perhaps some tea for our guest?"

Ramsay took a chair. "I thought you might like to know what happened."

"How did you get in?" Pauline asked. "We're supposed to have security."

"We've the right to come and go now we have a case," Ramsay replied. "The financial people can get warrants far easier than we can. In the modern world, corruption in the capitalist system is treated as the worst crime."

"Worse than murder?" Pauline teased.

Ramsay laughed. "There's no evidence of murder. But your point stands."

"So, you let Fenham go?"

"We had little choice," Ramsay said. "Your company may want an example made over an eighty-pound fraud, but the justice system has budgets to consider. The company can sue privately, at its own expense."

Pauline nodded. The thefts were pitifully small. "Fenham could have afforded the items from his salary. Why bother stealing? That's troubled me since the start."

"And your conclusion?"

"It's exactly what I'd expect from a petty man jealous of someone better liked. Using Neville's name to steal would be his final triumph -- disgracing Neville in senior management's eyes, while winning Violet with gifts. He never realised the gifts only made her unhappy and suspicious."

Ramsay nodded. "That's my view too. A mean-spirited man, bitter at his lot."

"I'm worried about Violet Paisley," Pauline said. "He's obsessed with her. She was seeing Neville too. I fear what he might do, though he's now apparently as charming as he can be toward her."

"He won't be stealing for her now that he knows we're watching," Ramsay said. "But you'll need to be clever to catch his next scheme."

"You think he murdered Neville too?" Pauline pressed.

"Judging by his character, yes," Ramsay admitted. "And if he wants revenge on Violet, there's not much any of us can do."

"Yes, there is," Pauline said firmly.

Ramsay became alarmed. He knew from experience Pauline's willingness to turn a dangerous criminal's attention to herself. "Miss Riddell, you know I can't approve of you making yourself a target. Find a group who can watch Violet round the clock. She's pretty. Plenty of young men will volunteer."

"That's a good idea," Pauline agreed. "And I know the man to organize it."

He chuckled. "While you're at it, arrange me an informal talk with Violet. She may know more about Fenham's gifts than you think."

"Brenda can arrange both," Pauline said. "You can use the meeting room, while I meet my new 'security chief' for Violet here in my office."

Once she had reassured Violet that Ramsay didn't bite and closed the meeting room door behind them -- with Brenda in attendance -- Pauline hurried back to her office, where Bob Wallace was waiting.

When Pauline apologized for pulling him away from work and explained, Bob laughed.

"My work is what I say it is, Miss Riddell. As for a team

to watch Violet, I could find a dozen. Every lad under twenty already watches her when she walks by."

"She is attractive," Pauline agreed. "But this must be more than lovesick boys. If the time comes, there may well be fisticuffs to protect her."

"The lads love a scrap," Bob said. "And Fenham would be a popular target. He's a sneaky rat, always informing for a step up the greasy pole."

"Can you get them started today?"

"Yes. I'll take the first shift. But what if she goes on a date with Fenham? We can hardly sit at the next table."

"He won't hurt her in public," Pauline replied. "Use your head."

Bob grinned. "It was just an example. Here's another, what if she goes into his home?"

"Pick bright lads, and they'll manage."

"It's on your head if they pick badly," Bob said. "Youngsters aren't always the most balanced."

"Better they jump too soon than too late."

Bob chuckled. "You just proved my point."

"Never mind, Bob. Just get it organized."

"You're prejudiced against him," Bob said. "Still, you may be right. You can count on me." He muttered as he left, "Wallace's Watchers?"

"The team's name isn't important, Bob," Pauline called after him, then noticed Violet leaving the meeting room, mascara streaking her cheeks.

Bob saw her too. His face hardened, but his tone as he replied to Pauline, was calm. "You'll find the name is often the most important part of morale." He went to Violet, took her arm, and led her away.

Pauline waited for Ramsay. She wanted to know why Violet was in tears, doubting Brenda would tell her.

She was right. Brenda returned first, furious and incoherent. Then Ramsay arrived, and Brenda stalked out.

"It didn't go well, I see," Pauline said.

"She was in tears from the moment she arrived," Ramsay said. "I'd hoped this setting would be easier than the station. But it looks as though we'll need her lawyer present next time. I could barely understand a word she said."

Knowing Violet, Pauline believed it. "Did you get anything?"

Ramsay shook his head. "Only that she neither stole, nor killed Neville. As I never thought she did, it takes us no further. Would Ethel Lambton be a better witness -- or must I drag them all down to the station?"

"I'll call her and ask," Pauline said. "You said she knows you, that might be enough."

Chapter Thirteen

PAULINE INVESTIGATES

Ethel entered Pauline's office and nodded to them both. Her greeting was as constrained as her expression. She barely acknowledged Ramsay when he reminded her they knew each other from chapel.

"As I explained on the phone," Pauline said, once Ethel had taken a chair at the end of her desk, "Inspector Ramsay would like to hear what you told me when we spoke."

Ethel nodded and turned to Ramsay. "I told Miss Riddell I knew nothing about purchase orders or invoices. I did the books for the 'club' before it became a department and supported them afterwards in a variety of roles. None of those involved purchasing spares or new parts." Her voice was flat, monotone. Pauline thought she'd rehearsed this statement many times on her way to the interview.

"You were the secretary though," Ramsay said, "so you must have had some knowledge of what was going on?"

Ethel's expression grew even more severe -- something Pauline hadn't thought possible. After a moment she said, "I was not trusted enough to join in with the boys and their everyday work. They asked for my help only when my knowledge was greater than theirs, and that was limited to highly technical electrical and electronic circuitry. I don't think the building burned down because of anything I advised on."

Ramsay smiled. "No, indeed. It appears to have been a bare wire on an electric kettle, which beggars belief. All those engineers, and something as basic as that was left unrepaired."

Ethel gave a short, sharp laugh. "I've noticed men will happily use damaged equipment they consider beneath their notice to replace. It doesn't surprise me at all."

"You aren't surprised by the fire?" Ramsay asked.

Ethel frowned. "You're twisting my words, Inspector. Of course I was surprised by the fire. What doesn't surprise me is that it came from such a source. I know how those boys operated. I doubt they even noticed the kettle flex was bare. Their heads were always in the clouds."

"You advised them but didn't join them?" Ramsay pressed.

"I wanted to be part of the Rocket Department, but my director wouldn't release me," Ethel said, her face flushing. "I was too important to lose, you see."

"That must have been frustrating," Ramsay suggested.

Ethel nodded, calmer now. "It was flattering to be so important to my department. However, I spoke to Neville, and we arranged this 'advisory position,' which my own department was also happy to accept."

Ramsay thanked her, and when she had gone, he turned to Pauline. "She doesn't give much away, does she?"

"She's like that all the time, Inspector. You can't assume it means she has something to hide," Pauline replied.

Ramsay nodded. "I last saw her when she was a teenager. She was prim and proper then and could quote scripture for any occasion. Chapel makes some people that way."

"Do you suspect her?" Pauline asked.

"I'm a policeman," Ramsay said with a grin. "I suspect everyone. But if Ethel had done it, it would have been in some fiendishly technical way we'd never dream of. On balance -- no."

Pauline smiled. "She would have liked to prove her superiority in the deed, I agree. I'm sorry for her though. Being thwarted in your work is always hard for people who have little life outside of it."

"She isn't thwarted though, is she?" Ramsay replied. "She's so important her boss wouldn't release her. I know she has patents and awards for her work -- they get mentioned in the local paper. She has plenty of acclaim."

Pauline frowned. "She wanted to lead the Rocket Department, and I'm sure she wants to head her current department too."

"And she won't, when the present boss leaves?" Ramsay asked.

Pauline shook her head. "She's not managerial material. Technically brilliant, personally inadequate. No one with real talent would stay in a department run by Ethel."

Ramsay nodded. "She certainly didn't shine in our interview just now."

"What comes next, Inspector?" Pauline asked.

"I'm meeting your Managing Director in fifteen minutes, then back to the station on another case. You?"

"I've an invoice trail to chase," Pauline said. "I should let my staff do it, but I can't. It's hard when you suspect everyone."

Ramsay laughed. "Welcome to the world of policing. Let me know if anything comes of your chase." He nodded goodbye.

Left alone, Pauline dug through the documents in the file she was building of Neville's final days. She retrieved the copy of the radio component purchase order that Neville had refused to sign off. As she passed Brenda she said, "I'm out. I'll get back to anyone who calls."

"Where will you be if I should need you?" Brenda asked, appalled at the idea of telling the Managing Director she didn't know.

"If you don't know, you won't be telling lies, will you," Pauline replied, closing the outer door firmly behind her. Her intention had been to search the Records vault but, on her way, another idea presented itself and she detoured to Naval Guns and Derek's office. He wasn't pleased to see her.

"What do you want?" Derek demanded.

"That night," Pauline said. "Was it just you and Neville?"

He nodded. "Yes. I told you. Col had been there earlier and left by the time Neville returned."

"No sign of anyone else?"

Derek frowned. "We saw no one. But we thought Col's soldering iron had been tampered with. And now we know the kettle wasn't as it should have been, so someone must have been there."

"Unless it was Col, before he left?" Pauline suggested.

"You don't know Col," Derek snapped. "Or you wouldn't say such things."

"He's above suspicion?" Pauline asked.

Derek nodded firmly. "Yes. I'd suspect myself before Col. Go talk to him. Then you'll see."

"I'll do that," Pauline said. "If he's as honest as you say, it will eliminate him from my investigation -- if you'll pardon the television police talk."

"Leave it to the real police," Derek told her. "That's what they're paid for."

Pauline agreed and left to search the vaults, as she had originally intended.

The elderly lady guarding the records vault was flustered when a senior manager demanded entry.

"My staff are busy," Pauline told her. "I need an answer right away." She smiled reassuringly, and the woman handed over the visitor register.

The documents were easy to find. The supporting paperwork was remarkably slim, but it gave her the address she needed. The delivery had been made to the Rocket Department loading bay and signed for with an illegible scrawl.

The guardian copied the document for Pauline, still nervous at the encounter. Pauline thanked her profusely to calm her nerves, then left for her office and her file of Fenham's signatures.

The samples were inconclusive. The scrawl didn't match Fenham's, but it didn't match the loading bay workers' either. Pauline frowned. Whoever picked up the part had hidden their identity well enough from an amateur such as herself. Could the police handwriting experts decipher it?

The paperwork also listed the shipper and its phone number. Pauline called the company and spoke to the owner. It was a small local firm, and the owner still answered the phone.

"Aye, I remember that load," he said, after Pauline explained her query.

"You do?"

"Aye. The order was to be delivered late, and I was to deliver it."

"That was unusual?" Pauline asked.

"I don't normally deliver to your company at all," he replied. "I can't say if it's unusual or not. I was just pleased to get an order that might get my foot in the door."

"Would you recognize the man you delivered to?"

"Nay. It were dark and cold. He had a hat and scarf covering most of his face. He looked like a regular loading bay man though."

"Did his voice sound different? An accent, perhaps?"

"Nay. Local, I'd say."

"Nothing to distinguish him?" Pauline pressed.

"Nothing. Like I said, it was dark and raining. I could see only his eyes and barely hear his voice." He paused, then added, "Oh! I forgot. He was wearing glasses."

"What kind? Expensive or plain?"

"The usual National Health ones. Wire-rimmed, round. Dark frames, but they all are, aren't they?"

"How tall was he?" Pauline demanded, her frustration rising. "Fat or skinny?"

The man laughed. "It were raining. He had on a heavy raincoat. I've no idea if he had a beer belly. As for height -- it was hard to tell. I didn't get out of the cab. He saw me coming, came out of the loading bay, and I handed the parcel through the window. He signed the form, and I left. Average height, maybe, but he was hunched against the rain."

Pauline thanked him and hung up. It could have been Fenham, or anyone else with access to purchase orders and the authority to tell Security a parcel was arriving late. The list of men who could do that wasn't long. And it was a man.

Her call to Security brought a promise of an investigation into that night's events and a report soon. With the police involved and memos circulating from the Managing Director, Security was keen to respond quickly to an Auditing request. They might still protect themselves, Pauline thought, but at least her investigation was moving.

By the time she had finished, Ramsay was back at her desk. "Well? Any joy?"

Pauline recounted what she had learned and what she was waiting to hear from Security.

"Then I'll wait, if you don't mind," Ramsay said, settling into a chair.

"Maybe some more tea?" Pauline suggested.

Ramsay grinned. "I thought you'd never ask."

Pauline requested Brenda to bring tea and biscuits for two. While she was gone, Pauline said, "We can talk freely for about ten minutes, no more."

"Then I'll ask why you're so sure Fenham is the murderer?"

"He has the best motive -- two motives, in fact. And he's a rat," Pauline said.

Ramsay frowned. "That's what I was afraid of. You're prejudiced against him, and that's dangerous for a detective."

"He fits every part of the story. He's head of Purchasing, most likely behind the thefts, and we know why. He had the most to lose if his thieving was exposed. He had a grudge against Neville. I could go on, but it won't convince you."

"On the contrary, you're probably right," Ramsay said with a grin. "But it's all those things that make me cautious. He's not a fool. He would have thought of this before he began and disguised it. My 'devil's advocate' side says he's being set up."

"Humph," Pauline began, then stopped as Brenda returned with the tray. While Ramsay moved to help her, Pauline considered his words. He had a point. Fenham may have been a rat, but never a fool. Was she missing the real murderer by focusing too much on him?

She was still wavering when the phone rang. It was Security. The person who had told them about the shipment that night was Morris Fenham.

"Ha!" Pauline cried, nearly making Brenda spill the tea. She covered the receiver and said, "Thank you, Brenda. I'll be mother -- you can get on." Once Brenda had left, Pauline told Security to repeat their news to Ramsay. Grinning, she handed him the phone and poured the tea while he listened.

"Now will you agree I'm right?" she demanded when he hung up.

"It's another point in your favor," Ramsay said. "But we've a way to go yet."

"You'll bring him in for questioning again?" Pauline pressed.

Ramsay laughed. "I'll ask him to escort me back to the station when I leave. Will that satisfy you?"

Pauline nodded. "And this time, don't let him go."

Chapter Fourteen

GOOD SUSPECT, SUSPECT AGAIN

Ramsay was only gone minutes when Violet appeared at Pauline's office asking to talk. Pauline agreed and, once Violet was inside, she told Brenda to refuse all calls and visitors, saying she was in conference.

"Has he been arrested?" Violet blurted the moment Pauline returned to her seat.

"No. He's just being taken in for further questioning," Pauline replied.

Violet was deflated. "Oh! He looked so frightened as he left the office, I thought he must have been arrested."

"You want him arrested?"

Violet nodded. "It's awful, I know. We shouldn't wish bad things to happen to others, but he frightens me."

"He seemed to be remarkably kind and gracious to you," Pauline said.

"He was too kind, much too kind," Violet replied. "It isn't natural. And when he talked or touched me, I could feel his anger inside." She shuddered.

"Did he threaten you?"

"No, but his 'suggestions,' his 'advice,' felt exactly like threats," Violet told her. "These past days have been terrifying. They will keep him in, won't they?"

Pauline chose her words carefully. "That will depend on his answers and the new evidence. Arresting people isn't always simple, especially when things are as confused as this." When she saw Violet's expression become even more dismal, she suggested, "Maybe you should have someone with you at all times."

Violet's expression shifted to puzzlement. "It's funny you should say that. Bob Wallace has been hanging around for the past hour. Every time I look up, there he is. He must agree with you."

Pauline smiled. "I'm pleased to hear that. It seems I'm not the only one worried about you."

"He's going to drive me home tonight and bring me in to work tomorrow," Violet continued. "And every day until Mr. Fenham is in prison, he says."

Pauline laughed. "Bob is getting ahead of himself. We really don't know if Morris Fenham is guilty. All we do know is he seems to have a split personality -- one part mean, and one part oily."

Violet nodded vigorously. "He's exactly like that. I'm sure now he isn't normal."

"Did he make you tell lies for him?" Pauline asked. "About what he was doing, perhaps?"

"Not exactly," Violet muttered, avoiding Pauline's eye. "He did remind me of when we were together and stuff like that."

"You didn't remember where you were?"

Violet squirmed. "I'm always busy so the times get confusing. He reminded me, that's all."

"Now you think he may not have been entirely honest

about the times and places?" Pauline asked.

Violet nodded unhappily.

"Did he mention being with you one evening back in the spring, for example?"

"Which evening?" Violet asked, puzzled.

"Any evenings," Pauline persisted.

"There were some evenings," Violet replied. "I don't remember the dates."

Pauline frowned. It was no more than she'd expected, but she'd hoped Fenham would have oversold his advice and given an exact date to a woman who couldn't, of her own accord, remember them. "Not one?"

Violet shook her head. "He just reminded me where and when, that's all."

"How did he do that without mentioning the dates?" Pauline asked, growing hopeful.

"Oh, he would say something like, 'on the day we had the party in the office for Hazel,'" Violet replied. "Things like that."

Pauline almost laughed at the simplicity of it all. Now all she needed to know was what happened in the Purchasing office on the day that radio component arrived. "Violet, would you do something for me?"

Violet looked doubtful. "If I can."

"Write down all the reminders he gave you and give the list to me later," Pauline said.

Violet's expression didn't change. "I don't remember many, but I'll try."

"Take your time," Pauline said. "With each one you write down, another will come back to you."

With this agreed, Pauline gently eased Violet out of the office, escorting her to the end of the corridor where she was pleased to see Bob casually reading a company notice-board that no one else ever read. She smiled, and he nodded in response.

After seeing Bob and Violet disappear back toward Purchasing, Pauline returned to her office.

Brenda pounced the moment Pauline entered the outer office. "What did she have to say?"

"She wanted to know if the police had arrested Mr. Fenham," Pauline replied. "I have a job for you, Brenda. It's part of the department's investigation, so I want you to be careful how you get this information."

Brenda's eyes lit up. "What do you need?"

"All the social or other events that took place in the Purchasing department from last November to now," Pauline said. "Anything that involved a celebration."

Brenda nodded. "Fenham was keen on that sort of thing. He said it was good for staff morale. The men hated it."

Pauline laughed. "They would," she said, remembering her brothers grumbling at every suggestion of a family party. "Anyway, whatever the staff remember, write it down and show no one. This might be the evidence we need to nail him."

"I'll do it," Brenda cried.

"Thank you," Pauline said. "Start now. I need the list right away -- or even earlier." She grinned as Brenda scurried out of her office, grabbing pencil and pad as she rushed into the corridor.

Back at her desk, Pauline picked up the file again. She began making a list of all the dates when parts were delivered. She suspected some of these would align with 'celebrations' in the Purchasing office, and some 'celebrations' would point to new avenues for investigation. Between the two, she'd have enough to expose all of Fenham's thieving

-- even if it didn't show when he made the leap to murder.

By the end of the workday, she had all three lists in hand. Violet's was the shortest, as she'd expected; her own list of dates came next; and Brenda's list of 'celebrations' was the longest. Now she had a job for Ian, the most energetic of her staff: check which parts arrived at the factory on the days the Purchasing department held celebrations.

After Brenda had found and delivered Ian to her office, she explained his mission. He nodded and asked, "Not just the Rocket Department then?"

"I suspect the Rocket Department is where this showed up because Neville was such a meticulous man. The other departments have been running for decades, and everyone is comfortable with the process. I doubt they look at the paperwork as closely as Neville did."

"When do you need this?" Ian asked.

"The police have Fenham in custody," Pauline said. "Ideally, I'd like the answer before they let him go."

Ian's expression was quizzical, but he nodded and left, saying, "Tell Security I'll be working late."

After speaking to Security, Pauline phoned Ramsay and left a message. He called back shortly after, and she explained her new research and her hope of having more evidence before the day was out.

"I'll hold him as long as I have something I'm allowed to hold him on," Ramsay reminded her. "I want a clean conviction here. I don't want it overturned by me doing something to sabotage that."

"Of course," Pauline said. "We're in violent agreement on this. I just want you to be aware more evidence might be coming."

"I hope so," Ramsay replied. "We're still only looking at

petty theft as the charge. We don't usually hold people overnight for that."

Pauline sat at her desk as the light outside began to fade. She didn't want to miss the moment when the evidence arrived. Finally, she couldn't wait any longer and hurried down to the vault, where she found Ian still diligently working his way through reams of documents.

"Anything?" Pauline asked.

"Not a lot," Ian admitted, "but maybe enough." He handed her a sheaf of papers, which she took to the nearest desk with a light.

Pauline flipped through them and smiled. She glanced at her watch. "I'm copying these and then phoning Inspector Ramsay. Keep going." She hurried off.

"Well, Miss Riddell?" Inspector Ramsay asked when she was put through to him.

"Well," Pauline replied, "we have new potential thefts, but we won't be able to confirm any of them tonight. I thought you should know."

"We have him wriggling over that evening delivery," Ramsay told her. "He says he did tell Security a delivery was arriving late, but he doesn't know anything about the radio equipment parts your people found. It was something quite different, a pressure gauge, he says, and it arrived the next day."

"It was just a coincidence this other delivery turned up? That's his story?" Pauline cried. "You can't believe that, surely."

"I don't. But until we investigate the deliveries that were scheduled for that day and confirm one was to be late, or not, and that it arrived the next day, or not, we can't keep holding him," Ramsay said. "I think, however, he'll run for it soon. He's sweating something awful."

"I hope you're right, because when he does, you'll have a reason to hold him," Pauline replied.

Ramsay laughed. "He'll guess that, so it won't be right away. Let me know what your new research shows."

"I'll have my whole staff on it first thing in the morning, and I'll tell him what we're doing if he's in work," Pauline said grimly. "Maybe that will make him try to escape."

Pauline's hope was misplaced. Her first visitor the following morning, even before she'd set her staff working on the new assignment, was Morris Fenham. He brushed past Brenda's objections, flung open Pauline's office door, and shouted, "I'm back."

"Good morning, Morris," Pauline replied, eyeing him coldly.

He stepped inside and slammed the door shut. "The problem you're having in your campaign against me is, I'm innocent." His expression was fixed in a manic smile that was more frightening than hate. His eyes blazed. His whole body vibrated with passion.

Pauline willed herself to answer calmly. "I have no campaign against you. I simply provide documents that have anomalies to senior management and, at their request, the police."

"Funny then it's me they keep interviewing and me they keep accusing," Fenham shouted.

He was dangerously close now, and she could feel, smell, his breath on her face. He'd been drinking. Pauline's hand reached for the phone, but he slammed his own hand down on it.

"Forget that," Fenham snarled. They were almost nose-to-nose now. "I'm telling you to stop. I didn't kill Halliday or burn down the rocket building."

"But you have used the company's money to buy gifts for Violet and maybe yourself," Pauline replied, refusing to step back, though the smell of whisky on his breath nauseated her.

He seemed genuinely amused when he responded. "Are you kidding? Half the people here walk out every night with as much. Are you investigating them?"

"A pen, a pad of paper, some scrap metal for their garden shed," Pauline retorted. "None of this comes close to what you seem to have taken these past months."

"Everyone takes stuff, and not just once," he growled. "If it isn't every day, it's damn close. It adds up. Do you think I'd risk my job, my salary, my pension for some silly trinkets for Violet or anyone?"

"Then how do you explain the items we're finding?" Pauline demanded, her anger growing the more he denied the evidence.

"I'm being framed, you stupid woman," he yelled. "Or are you so blind you can't see the obvious?"

Pauline found herself once again brought up short. Ramsay too had suggested she was being too narrowly focused. Was she?

"Cat got your tongue?" Fenham quipped sarcastically. "You hadn't thought of it at all, had you? You really are stupid."

He's the manager of Purchasing. He'd have made his embezzlement harder to find than what they'd seen, Pauline thought, her insides in knots.

"If you're being framed, we'll discover it," she said, calmer now. "The truth will come out."

This made things significantly worse. His rage became a physical presence in the room; it hardly seemed part of him anymore. "You're mad! With you pouring oil on the fire, it will only come out when I'm in prison, or homeless on the street, or just plain dead."

Pauline reddened. "I'll have my staff dig deeper. We'll review everything we've found through the lens of you being framed. If you are, we'll find out and show by whom."

Her words had the effect she wanted. Quieter now, he asked, "And tell others that's what you're doing?"

"We will make it clear we're keeping an open mind and examining all possibilities," Pauline replied. "If someone is behind this, I don't want them escaping before we have the evidence."

"If someone runs, that will confirm their guilt," he argued. "Isn't that what we all want?"

Pauline nodded. "Very well. We will explicitly say we're considering the possibility someone is framing you. I don't want to limit it to just that, however."

He nodded. "Do that and stop picking on me," Fenham said, and turned away. Before he reached the door, it opened, and a Security officer entered.

"Is everything all right here, Miss Riddell?" the man asked, glaring at Fenham.

"It is, thank you," Pauline replied, smiling. "Mr. Fenham has some concerns and was quite vocal about them, that's all."

The security officer stood aside while Fenham left, then said, "It might be wise not to be alone when you walk to and from your car, Miss Riddell -- if he's as 'vocal' as you say."

Pauline thanked him for his advice and sat down. Now it was over, her legs were wobbly, and her heart was racing.

Brenda stepped in. "I thought it best to phone Security.

I hope that was right. Fenham stormed past me and wouldn't take no for an answer."

Pauline nodded. "He didn't hurt you, did he?"

Brenda shook her head. "My old man would have something to say to him, if he had."

"Then I think we should mark this in our desk diaries, in case something comes of it," Pauline told her. "But otherwise, do our best to put it out of our minds."

In this she was successful -- until it came time to leave at the end of the day, when she could see from the window that her car was practically alone in the park and there was no one in the yard. Where was Fenham?

Chapter Fifteen

IT IS MURDER

Inspector Ramsay studied the Safety Investigation report he'd been given earlier, though it was incidental to his own investigation -- and there'd be trouble if Gregson learned of his prying. The report didn't say anything vastly different from the Fire Department's version, except in one respect. The fire report had said the blaze began at the frayed cable of the electric kettle and released dangerous chemicals from the cloth it was wrapped in. The Safety Report, however, said the fumes from those chemicals had knocked Neville out long before the smoke had filled his office. It also implied that the cloth, the chemicals, and the frayed cable likely weren't an accident because not all the chemicals involved were stocked in the rocket building.

He phoned the report's author and, when connected, asked, "Couldn't the cloth have been brought in from another building?"

"Of course it could," the man replied. "Still, the coincidence of having this saturated cloth in the one place where a bare cable was going to be energised is suspicious."

104

"What sort of person might have known about this combination?" Ramsay asked. "For instance, I'd know a bare cable could start a fire and that a cloth placed there would likely burn, but I wouldn't know which chemicals to soak into the cloth."

The author considered. "I'd say a lot of the technical staff at the factory would know -- engineers, scientists, those kinds of people."

Ramsay grunted. "That doesn't narrow it down much. The factory is full of 'those kinds of people.'"

The man laughed. "A lot, yes, but not the whole factory. Out of the thousands working there, I'd say probably a hundred at most."

"Only a hundred," Ramsay said dryly. "Thanks. We'll start interviewing them right now and have an answer by Christmas."

"That's your job, Inspector," the man retorted. "Mine was to give you the facts and possible avenues to explore."

With the conversation over, Ramsay considered what to do. The answer was to delegate it to the new man he'd been given while Morrison was away at Police College. He'd hoped never to give the youngster anything before Morrison returned, but the boy had some kind of higher-education certificate, and here, where educated people were thick on the ground, perhaps he might prove useful.

Rising to his feet, Ramsay ambled out of his office to find Detective-Constable Urmston, who was making his morning tea when the Inspector descended on him.

"I have a job for you," Ramsay said, "right up your street." He explained what he wanted while the young man listened intently. "Any questions?"

"A list of technically trained people at the factory who had dealings with the Rocket Department, and any possible motives they might have for wishing it harm," Urmston replied. "It's a big factory, sir, and there will be many different universities to contact for details. This will take time."

"Then you shouldn't wait to get started," Ramsay told him. "Prioritise those closest to the rockets and work outwards. Give me what you learn as you go."

"Right, sir," Urmston said, grinning.

To Ramsay, the assignment sounded like a nightmare, but Urmston seemed eager. "Then let me have something by the end of the day, Constable," Ramsay said, dismissing him.

Do I tell Miss Riddell about this new avenue? Ramsay thought. And what about Neville's second-in-command, Derek? Maybe he should be first on Urmston's list. Ramsay turned back, found the constable, and gave him Derek Parker as his first subject. With that done, he returned to the question of what to tell Miss Riddell.

Meanwhile, Pauline had returned to her office without being molested by anyone. She quickly called her staff together and directed them to consider the possibility that Fenham was being framed.

"Didn't someone say that 'anything's possible in this, the best of all possible worlds?'" Ian asked derisively. "Everything I'm seeing says it's him."

Fred retorted, "If he is being framed, that's exactly what it will look like. Otherwise, the plan would be useless."

John agreed, but added, "On the other hand, he could have made this so obvious as a double bluff. Maybe his plan was always to fall back on the 'being framed' story."

"All I'm asking," Pauline told them, "is that we look out for some oddity suggesting he's being framed. If he is, we find it. That way he and we have a solid relationship in the future. If we don't, and he is innocent, we've made a bad enemy."

The murmur of agreement suggested mixed feelings about this added task. They left in silence, and Pauline returned to her office to follow her own instructions. Could she find anything in the documents that supported Fenham's claim?

Ramsay's call, shortly after, multiplied her uneasiness about her role in Fenham's harassment.

"If what you say is true," she told him, when he finished outlining the report's disturbing suggestion, "then it's unlikely to be Fenham. He's always been on the financial side. He'd know a bare wire could cause a fire -- we all know that -- but the bit about a cloth soaked in chemicals would be beyond him."

"We may be looking at two separate crimes that have only come to light because one was wrapped up inside the other," Ramsay suggested.

"A murderer and an embezzler suddenly appearing out of nowhere, and at the same time, is quite a coincidence, Inspector."

"The one crime may go back months, even years, and be spread throughout the factory," Ramsay argued. "The other happened because the Rocket Department, or just Neville, stepped on someone's toes. Not as strange as it might sound."

Pauline recounted Fenham's rage the previous day and how his performance, which should have convinced her of guilt, instead made her question if he wasn't being framed.

"You thought his anger was genuinely about his innocence in the face of repeated questioning?" Ramsay asked.

"I did. He was furious and desperate to be given a fair hearing," Pauline admitted. "I believed him."

"Was it the murder or the embezzlement that was upsetting him?"

"It was hard to be sure," Pauline replied. "At the time, I thought just the embezzlement. I thought it hurt his professional pride that we thought him so stupid in his criminality. He was angry because we should have assumed he wasn't to blame -- the documentation was so easily found and linked to him, if you see what I mean."

"I do," Ramsay replied with a laugh. "If I committed a murder, I hope I'd make a better fist of hiding it than he appears to have done with his financial jiggery-pokery."

"Exactly," Pauline cried. "And now you tell me it looks unlikely he could have manufactured the murder, which makes me think I've got the wrong perpetrator. I've jumped to the easy conclusion, and I should have known better."

"You're out of practice, Miss Riddell," Ramsay teased.

"Possibly," Pauline admitted. "But I'm going to be much more careful about what we pass on to you from now on. Have your financial investigators found anything?"

"Even if they had," Ramsay retorted, "they wouldn't tell me. Don't waste your energies wondering if they're finding wrongdoing. They're looking at stocks, shares, bonds, loans, foreign-exchange irregularities -- all the things nobody at our level ever sees."

"I feel sorry for our MD then," Pauline said. "I fear his decision to root out wrongdoing by taking this to the authorities will come back to bite him. The Board members won't forgive him unless something is found, or nothing is found, and we get a clean bill of financial health. Maybe not even then."

"You'll never get a 'clean bill of health,'" Ramsay said. "It isn't how these people work. There'll always be doubts, concerns, innuendoes, insinuations, every kind of subtle smear in their report."

Pauline groaned. "I hope you're wrong. Our Managing Director gave me my start and this department to run."

"I've been wrong before," Ramsay chuckled. "Maybe my cynicism is misjudged, and all will be well."

Returning to the point, Pauline said, "If it isn't Fenham, then Bob protecting Violet is a waste of effort."

"And if it is, he's right to be concerned," Ramsay replied. "Let things run their course until we have a result."

"We have to be quicker," Pauline argued. "The damage being done to the company and its management won't easily be repaired. And Violet won't be willing to keep herself safe forever."

"You look out for your own safety," Ramsay warned. "Let Violet look after hers."

Pauline chuckled. "I have a stiletto-style paperknife I now carry in my pocket. You didn't hear that if you're called to a stabbing death in the coming days."

He agreed he hadn't heard her say anything about knives and rang off. Pauline smiled. She could tell by his response he was concerned, and she suspected she'd soon notice a man shadowing her whenever she was outside work.

Chapter Sixteen

A NEW SUSPECT

The factory siren sounded, and the workers began streaming out of the gates, which meant the office staff had another hour before the end of their workday. Pauline watched them from her office window and wondered if among them was someone so angry at Neville that they wanted to kill him. But why? What could Neville have done that would warrant such an action? Another one of Violet's many admirers, perhaps? As she thought this, Pauline began to smile. Poor Violet. She was a harmless, rather silly girl, yet she was being imagined as a dangerous femme fatale by a very amateur sleuth.

Leaving the window, Pauline paced the office restlessly. She wanted to see that Violet was being escorted when she left, and the best way to do that wasn't from the office window. It was to be down near where Violet worked at quitting time. Pauline glanced at her watch, then went out to Brenda and asked for a reminder just before home time.

Puzzled, Brenda agreed and set her watch on the desk in front of her. Pauline returned to her own desk and did the same. It was the longest hour of her life; she could feel the minute hand ticking slowly toward the half hour.

Brenda looked around the door. "Almost time, Boss."

Pauline thanked her and, replacing her watch on her wrist, left for the Typing Pool office, where she arrived just in time to see the typists covering their typewriters and gathering their belongings under the stern, watchful eye of the elderly supervisor.

Pauline was still pretending to read memos on the notice board when Bob Wallace appeared at her side. She greeted him with relief. The absence of anyone else waiting had begun to alarm her.

Bob grinned. "I do the journey to and from the factory with my car. I've got three other lads to cover the remaining hours. Don't worry. She'll be quite safe."

Pauline nodded, though still anxious. "In a way, it's wrong of us to do this. Violet isn't a child. We shouldn't be minding her."

Bob shrugged. "In normal times, it would be wrong. These aren't normal times. If, as we suspect, he's killed once because of Violet, he may well kill her now she's rejected him again."

Before she could reply, the door burst open, and the typists began to stream out. When they saw Bob, they laughed.

"Violet," one called. "Your new fancy man is here."

There was general laughter, and Bob flushed red, doubling their mirth.

"Don't listen to them, Bob," Violet said, arriving at his side and sliding her hand inside his arm. "They're just jealous." She smiled at Pauline. "Hello, Miss Riddell. I hope you weren't trying to have Bob all to yourself?"

"I was just passing and stopped to talk," Pauline replied. "Goodnight, both of you."

"Was that a hint, do you think?" Violet asked Bob, with an inviting smile, as she led him away.

Pauline didn't hear Bob's undoubtedly convoluted reply as they left. Poor Bob, she thought on her way to the stairs. *I hope he learns to cope with her flirting, or she'll come to despise him for not picking up on her cues.*

Pauline turned back to the question of who'd killed Neville, if not Fenham. She knew nothing of Neville's life outside work -- or indeed much about him at all. She needed to find Derek; he would know. Fortunately, he was just leaving his office when she arrived there, and he agreed to talk as they walked.

"I don't want to spend one minute longer than I have to in this place," he told her.

Knowing he would never have the job he wanted, Pauline wisely chose not to acknowledge the remark. Instead, she asked, "Could Neville have made enemies outside work, perhaps with someone who also works here?"

"We all make enemies, Miss Riddell, but not the murdering kind," Derek replied. "Neville lived for his rockets. He barely saw or spoke to anyone else, so I think it unlikely he made this kind of enemy."

"Maybe one of his rockets landed in someone's allotment and broke their greenhouse?" Pauline suggested. "That's a foolish example, but you see what I mean."

He nodded. "I do. But all the rockets I remember landed out to sea. None came down on land. We were careful about that. Sometimes dog walkers were angry about the launches frightening their pets. It never amounted to more than a few cross words. After all, launches only last a few seconds."

"What about you?" Pauline asked, trying to shake him out of his sullen refusal to fight for his place in the company.

"Me?"

"Neville had the job you would die for," Pauline said. "Would you kill for it?"

"You're mad," Derek replied, though without any heat. "I only had the job I had because Neville could talk the legs off a donkey. He got that from his mother. She's Irish and must've kissed the Blarney Stone. What a talker she is!"

By now, they'd reached Derek's BSA Rocket motorcycle, and he began fastening his helmet.

"There's nothing you can think of?" Pauline tried one last time, as he straddled the machine and kicked it into life.

"Nothing," he shouted above the roar of the engine. With a wave, he slipped the bike into gear and rode away.

Pauline returned to her office to find Ian just turning from it.

"You have something?" she cried, hope springing in her heart.

He nodded. "But not about Fenham, though he could still be involved."

"Come in," Pauline said, leading the way inside. When they were seated, she continued, "Tell me."

Ian handed over a number of orders and invoices. "These are more of the scrawled signature we haven't matched. See?"

Pauline examined them. She nodded. "I do see."

"Now look at this," Ian said, handing her a memo to the men of Rocket Department about safety equipment.

Pauline saw it at once. The signature was readable this time, but the scrawl they hadn't identified shared all the same elements. It was Bob Wallace's signature.

"We'll need the police handwriting expert to confirm it," Pauline said slowly. "I don't understand."

"I think they were in it together," Ian suggested. "Having one in the Rocket Department and one in Purchasing would make the swindle so much simpler."

"But Bob?" Pauline cried. "He's one of the nicest men I know."

"Before we say anything, we must have this analysed," Ian insisted. "We can't get this wrong. Everyone likes Bob. He's one of the good ones."

Pauline nodded, her stomach in knots, her mind in turmoil. "I'm taking these around to Inspector Ramsay right now," she said, leaping to her feet.

"Make copies," Ian warned. "Those are the originals, and likely the only ones. If they go missing, we'd have to start again."

Using the mimeograph copier at Brenda's desk, Pauline ran off two sets and handed the originals back to Ian. "Put these back in the vault and keep our copy safe. I've only just realised I've seen Bob at the vault more than once. He was probably looking to find and destroy these."

"Then these might actually be the last of them," Ian said. "Every other one may already be gone."

Pauline nodded. "Make another copy for the vault and leave me the originals." With that done, she put on her coat and set out for her car. It was raining heavily, and for that she was glad. Few people would see her in the downpour.

Ramsay was still at the police station when she arrived -- as she knew he would be. He'd told her more than once, 'he didn't have a home to go to, only a house'.

"It will be tomorrow before our expert can examine these," Ramsay told her. "But they look the same. Same enough for me, anyway."

Pauline almost screamed with impatience at another day lost. Violet could be murdered before they knew the truth. Bob Wallace, of all people. And he was sweet on Violet too. Was he a threat as well?

She returned to her own 'house not a home' in a dismal mood, wishing she knew where any of the people concerned lived. Looking in the phone book for Violet, she tried the two names listed under "Paisley," only to discover they had no idea who she was talking about. "You'd think they'd be related," she muttered when the second one denied knowing Violet.

Work the next morning was equally galling. Pauline arrived early enough to see Bob arrive with Violet. After parking his car, they walked to the offices, Violet once again holding his arm. Bob wore a pleased, bemused expression that made Pauline's heart ache. No matter what happened today, she couldn't see this ending happily for the Rocket Department foreman.

Almost immediately after, she saw Ian sprint across the yard to the office doors. Moments later, he burst into her office, gasping for breath.

"You ran up the stairs, I assume," Pauline said, grinning.

He nodded, still catching his breath. Once able to speak, she reassured him she'd done as promised: the originals were with the police.

"I hardly slept last night worrying about these documents," Ian admitted. "I imagined all sorts of things going wrong, even though I'd placed copies back in the vault."

"Then there's nothing we can do but wait," Pauline said, and Ian took himself off to his office, leaving her with only paperwork. For once, she almost wished for a meeting. Her staff, at least, were still combing through thousands of documents in the vault.

She phoned her boss and got his secretary, who said, "The MD is at a meeting all morning. He won't be back until the afternoon. Will you leave a message?"

Pauline thanked her and asked for a personal meeting. The secretary granted her fifteen minutes at one o'clock, warning her not to be late. Pauline and the woman had never hit it off. Reflecting on why, Pauline decided it was because the secretary loved her boss and thought Pauline a rival.

Late morning, her phone rang. She beamed with relief when she heard Ramsay's voice.

"Our expert says, 'well spotted,'" Ramsay confirmed. "Not everyone would have seen the points."

Pauline confessed it was Ian who had first noticed and asked, "Have you enough to arrest him?"

"Enough to bring him in for questioning," Ramsay replied. "I'll do that this morning. Have you told your boss?"

Pauline explained.

"Then I'll wait until you do," Ramsay said. "I don't imagine Mr. Wallace is likely to run when he doesn't know we're on to him."

A cold shiver ran through Pauline. "He might," she exclaimed. "We put copies back in the vault last night. If he finds them, he might guess we know."

"Then I'll put officers on the factory gates, and you can tell the boss why," Ramsay told her, laughing.

"I wish I'd never become involved," Pauline grumbled. "I like Bob Wallace, and now I find he's a murderer."

"We don't know that," Ramsay replied. "But if it isn't Fenham, your friend Wallace is the most likely alternative. Though I find it as puzzling as you do."

"He's besotted with Violet," Pauline said. "He hid it well

until now. Now he can't stop grinning like the Cheshire Cat."

"Neville must have really upset Violet to make someone want to murder him," Ramsay said. "But if Neville's behavior had made someone so upset, why wasn't Violet mad at him too?"

"Maybe Bob will explain everything when you question him," Pauline replied. "Violet's the reason, I'm sure of that, but why, I can't explain."

Chapter Seventeen

NEW SUSPECT RELEASED

After her talk with Ramsay, Pauline got on with her work by calling a meeting with her staff. They had an impressive pile of documents, going back over a year, that looked like they might be part of Fenham's scheme. There were very few, Pauline noted, with the possible Bob Wallace forgeries. If she was right, Bob had removed almost all of them before Ian found some of the last remaining documents.

"Ian told us what he found, and I haven't seen anything like those," Fred assured her, when she posed the question. John agreed.

Ian added, "I've been thinking about this. If he can remove them like he's doing, then his thefts may not have been part of Fenham's scheme. He may have been acting alone. I didn't see anywhere Wallace wrote the purchase order and Fenham signed the delivery slip, for example."

Pauline frowned. When Ramsay reminded her that the evidence she'd provided wasn't conclusive, it awakened her to her own failings. She'd run ahead of the evidence, thinking Bob was the murderer -- far ahead of it. For all she knew, the signatures could be forged. This realisation, thankfully not public, made her cheeks flush pink.

"We'll have Brenda mimeograph what you've found and hand the copies over to the police," Pauline told them. "Meanwhile, we should finish our internal investigation and provide the boss with a report he can take to the Board."

"What about the police's financial investigators?" Fred asked.

Pauline recounted Ramsay's explanation to her, adding, "We're doing the internal investigation, and we need to have evidence and recommendations for stopping this happening again to the Managing Director by the end of this week. He's phoning me daily asking when he can see some results."

"Then we need more people," Ian protested. "There are thousands, maybe tens of thousands, of records each year. I've only done one year so far."

Pauline shook her head. "For the purposes of this report, one year is enough. Older frauds can wait."

"Then I can have my findings and recommendations to you today," Ian said.

The other two nodded. "The same," Fred said, acting as spokesman for the two older men.

She thanked them and went in search of the MD, who said, "I'm pleased to hear it. The Board is getting testy and threatening a change of leadership if they aren't informed soon of the steps I'm taking to fix this problem."

"I'll have it to you tomorrow," Pauline assured him. "You can tell them we haven't found any major losses. Just a steady outflow of fairly small amounts for radio and other electronic equipment, along with some small gift items. It won't significantly affect the bottom line on this year's profit and loss accounts."

"If it's as small as you say, why did he do it?" the MD asked.

Pauline said, "For that, we'll need the police to get answers. I'd be happy to throw him in a dungeon until he talks, but we can't do that nowadays."

Her boss nodded. "Sadly, it is frowned on in today's polite company. Very well, tomorrow. Don't be late."

Pauline was making her way to the staff canteen when she saw Bob Wallace re-entering through the factory gate. She went to meet him.

"Hello, Bob. I see the police have released you."

He nodded. "Despite your betrayal, I only 'helped them with their inquiries'. Isn't that the phrase they use?"

"My 'betrayal', as you phrase it, consisted of handing over documents my department found in the vault," Pauline replied. "Did someone watch Violet for us?"

"Yes, I had time to get one of the lads to take my place," Bob said. "Obviously you didn't think to do it."

Feeling a little guilty that she hadn't thought to do so, Pauline walked with Bob back toward the canteen.

"You were able to show them those scrawls were not your signature?" There seemed little point in pretending she didn't know why he'd been taken for questioning.

"I didn't have to," he replied. "They were clearly forgeries, and I told them so. Unless they can show they aren't, they have no reason to keep me in custody. My lawyer made that plain to their senior officers, and here I am."

"Who might have forged your signature, Bob?" Pauline asked, as he opened the canteen door for her.

"How should I know?"

"It didn't remind you of anyone's handwriting?" Pauline asked, as they made their way to the serving station.

He laughed. "Mine, to be fair. They were good forgeries. Though I'd never have done that scrawl they showed me. Looked more like a doctor's writing than a regular person's."

Taking a tray from the pile, and placing a plate and cutlery on it, Pauline continued, "You didn't order parts for the Rocket Club at all?"

Bob frowned. "Course I did. I'm General Foreman in the Rocket Department. I often bought materials and parts we needed. I'm sure your boys will find plenty of purchase orders with my name on them -- and some delivery slips with my signature on them. Just not those ones you gave the police. They were forgeries. More of Morris Fenham's handiwork, I'd say."

"We shouldn't accuse people, Bob," Pauline said as she placed salad items on her plate, while he piled potatoes, steak and kidney pudding, carrots, and gravy on his. "We must follow the evidence and let the police decide."

Bob grunted. "Then they should hurry up. I don't want them accusing me of wrongdoing again."

"They must interview people, Bob. How else can they learn what's true and what's false?" They paid and found a table.

"I'm glad you were able to confirm those signatures weren't yours," Pauline told him, when they were seated. "We've worked so well together on this investigation."

"Perhaps, then, you should have asked me before you gave those documents to the police," Bob replied.

Pauline shook her head. "We can't do that. I'm sure you can see why."

He shrugged. "I suppose. It's still not nice."

"It isn't," Pauline agreed. "One of the bad parts of auditing is uncovering mistakes and putting innocent people under a microscope."

"These weren't mistakes," Bob growled. "Someone was out to frame me."

"But who?"

"I've told you, and your reply was I shouldn't accuse people," Bob replied. "Make up your mind."

"We were at the serving station," Pauline said, looking around anxiously. "We mustn't let others know what we're thinking."

Bob snorted. "He's been hauled into the police station at least twice; everyone knows he's guilty of something."

Pauline nodded. "And we mustn't do anything to prejudice a case against him. Why would he frame you?"

This sudden continuation of her question seemed to set Bob back at first. Then he said, "Because I made my feelings about Violet known to him. He took it badly."

"I see," Pauline said. "When was this?"

Bob shrugged. "Last year sometime. When he first started bothering her. I can't give you a date. November, maybe?"

This did tie in with the dates on the documents Ian had found. The trouble was, Ramsay would have shown Bob those documents during the interview, and now Bob was repeating what he'd seen back to her. None of this helped clear him, in Pauline's mind. Had Bob decided to discredit Fenham by running a small, amateurish set of phony purchase orders that Fenham's group might pay, giving the impression it was Fenham who was using Bob's name? Allowing Bob to point the finger at Fenham when the time came? Getting Fenham sacked and driven out of town? It seemed crazy -- only no crazier than the scheme Fenham himself was already using.

Her staff delivered their reports by mid-afternoon, and Pauline began on her own. She had a first draft ready by the time everyone had gone, and the offices were quiet. Only the sounds of old buildings settling in for the long chilly night occasionally disturbed her. Pushing the report aside, she rose to stretch her legs and back. She made her way to the window and looked out. Her car was there, and so was one other. Her stomach flipped. It looked like Fenham's. Taking her office door key from her desk, she quickly locked herself in. If she recognised his car, she was sure he would recognise hers.

The silence now was oppressive. Each creak and groan alarmed her, and it took considerable effort to remain calm. Footsteps in the corridor set her heart racing, and she grabbed the handset, prepared to phone security. Her laugh when she saw the security guard peering in the door was so nervous, she couldn't deny she was rattled. She waved for him to wait. Unlocking the door, she asked if he'd escort her to her car. He agreed, and Pauline swept all the papers on her desk into her briefcase and followed him out of her office.

She was not surprised when Fenham left his own office the moment he saw her descending the stairs.

"Working late, I see, Miss Riddell," he said as he joined her on the final flight of stairs to the ground. "And wisely having an escort too," he continued, smiling at the security officer. "On these dark nights, it's best to be safe. I hope you won't mind if I join you."

As he was already alongside when he said this, Pauline could hardly object.

"I hope you and the police have given up harassing me," Fenham continued, as if discussing the weather. "I'm contemplating suing, you see. If you've turned your attention to Bob Wallace, a much more suitable candidate, I might consider forgetting all I've suffered at your hands."

"Why do you say Bob is a more suitable candidate?" Pauline asked.

Fenham laughed. "He's always snooping about where he has no business being. Or hadn't you noticed?"

"That's true," Pauline agreed. "I often see him in your department's vaults. I assumed he had permission."

"Oh, he does," Fenham replied. "But he is there more than his position warrants. I've been meaning to mention it to you since you began this investigation of yours. Then I was taken in for questioning, and I realised it would look bad on me, pointing the finger at someone else."

"And now the police have questioned Bob, it's open season on him?"

Fenham looked pained. "Miss Riddell, I've suggested to you only once, just now, that he is in and out of our vault more than I think he should be, and you choose to interpret that as me declaring 'open season' on him? You see now why I said nothing before."

They'd reached Pauline's car by this time, and she agreed she may have exaggerated a little. Thanking him for his observation, she wished him good night, before jumping into her car out of the cold wind that threatened rain was on the way.

She drove home watching the lights in her rear-view mirror, hoping that each set she saw was not Fenham following her. When she parked in the narrow drive of her house, she looked about to see if she was being watched. Nobody seemed to be nearby, and the threatened rain had arrived, blotting out much of the view. She exited her car and scurried into the house, locking and bolting the door behind her.

It was midnight before her report was finished. She'd rewritten the findings a dozen times or more before she was happy with it. Embezzlement by person, or persons, unknown was what she'd said, and that's how it must stay until the police finished their investigation. The recommendations to prevent this happening again were much simpler to write.

Chapter Eighteen

OLD SUSPECT NEW AGAIN

Brenda had the report typed and copied by nine o'clock. The moment she handed over the original, Pauline hurried to the executive suite and delivered it directly to her boss's secretary.

"Be sure he gets this the moment he arrives, please," Pauline instructed, fixing the woman with a stony glare. "He's been waiting for this."

The secretary returned Pauline's gaze coolly. "I know how much he wants to see it," she replied, unconcerned.

Pauline nodded and left, promising herself she would phone the Managing Director the instant she saw his car arrive. On her way back to her office, however, she detoured into Fenham's office and told him the report was finished 'and in the MD's hands.' Not strictly true, but Pauline felt no guilt about the white lie.

"Shouldn't you have run that by me first?" Fenham demanded. "After all, it's my department."

"If the boss wants you to see it, you will," Pauline

replied curtly, and strode out. She smiled grimly to herself. Now let's see who he runs to.

She lingered near the toilets at the end of the corridor, hoping to witness some dramatic fallout, but if Fenham contacted anyone, he did so by phone. Cursing the modern world and its stifling technology, she returned to her office, where she learned the MD had already called for her. Grimacing at her own wasted time, she hurried to his office.

"Person, or persons, unknown, eh?" he remarked when she entered.

"I couldn't do otherwise until we hear from the police," Pauline replied, settling into the chair he indicated.

"How much will these improvements cost?" he demanded.

"We only have preliminary figures for a new purchasing system, and they're prohibitive, in my opinion. I'd recommend limiting the authority to write purchase orders, adding additional signature checks, and revising departmental coding for now."

He nodded. "Pleased to hear it."

He read silently for a moment before looking up. "Can we be sure enough it is Morris Fenham?"

Pauline hesitated. "There's some evidence to suggest another person may be involved."

"Not working alone then?"

"Possibly. There may have been two people buying for their own use."

"You think someone saw what Fenham was doing and started their own little sideline?"

Pauline grew uneasy. She'd been chosen for this role because years ago she'd spotted financial irregularities in a report she was typing and had later helped the police bring murderers to justice. Her boss had been impressed enough to promote her and sponsor her through university for an accounting degree. Now she found herself hedging with 'possibly', 'probably', and 'there may have been'... She didn't like the bureaucratic tone creeping into her work.

"We don't yet have enough evidence to say who, how many, or whether they were working together," she admitted at last.

"The police aren't getting anywhere either," her boss grunted. "Even Halliday's death seems beyond them. They can't say if it was an accident, manslaughter, or murder."

"The fire destroyed all the evidence," Pauline reminded him.

"So I understand," he said, unimpressed. "I wanted the police involved to make an example of the culprit -- or culprits. We're cracking down on thefts among the blue-collar staff and I won't tolerate less with the white-collar ones. These crooks are bleeding us dry."

Pauline reminded him, "The company looked the other way in better times. It became a perk of working here, and you know that."

"Which is why it must end fairly, for everyone. Now get me names and evidence that will stick, because the police clearly won't."

Pauline kept her expression neutral. Unlike the police, she had no means of forcing confessions. If her suspects denied everything, what then?

"Very well. May I have permission to pay my staff over-time? There are thousands of records and only four of us."

He shook his head. "They can have extra time off at the end if they deliver results. Overtime is out of the question."

After some haggling, she extracted a better promise of compensatory leave, then returned to her office. She gath-ered her team and outlined the task: they were to review every purchase decision for the past two years. "That includes you, Brenda, if you'll help."

Brenda was enthusiastic. Fred looked least pleased—Pauline suspected he preferred not to spend extra hours at home with his wife, but the promise of extra time off over Christmas and New Year swayed him.

"One of you show Brenda what you're doing," Pauline said. "I'll help when I can. We must find something that can't be argued away."

Her staff had only just left when Derek knocked and entered.

"Yes?" Pauline asked cautiously. She wasn't sure he wasn't a suspect himself.

"What did you say to Fenham this morning?" Derek asked, grinning with delight.

"Why?"

"He came barreling into Naval Guns and harangued Bob Wallace for fifteen minutes."

"Why do you think I had anything to do with that?"

"Because minutes earlier, I saw you in Fenham's office. He was clearly furious, and he got on the phone the moment you left…"

"Who to?"

Derek frowned. "How should I know? I was watching from the corridor, not hiding under his desk."

"Of course. Go on."

"When he finished ranting, he stormed out of Bob's office, cursing the world. It was a treat to watch."

"And what did Bob do?" Pauline asked.

"He shouted right back, nose-to-nose. Then, after Fenham left, Bob phoned someone. And no, I don't know who. I was watching from my broom cupboard. Did I mention Bob got a better office than I did?"

Pauline barely heard the complaint. She was busy thinking: There's someone else in this. A Mr. X. But who?

"Thanks, Derek," she said. "I wanted to know what Fenham would do after I told him the report was with the boss."

"What he did was make it clear Wallace is in it with him," Derek said. "Everyone in our office is talking of nothing else."

"It seems like it," Pauline agreed. "But it isn't hard evidence, which is what we need."

"I'll get that," Derek promised. "If those two killed Neville, I want to hear they've swung for it."

"Steady, Derek. It may have been accident or manslaughter, not murder."

Derek shrugged. "If they're responsible, I want justice. That's it."

"What will you do first?" Pauline asked.

"Edie on the switchboard will know who Wallace and Fenham called. She might even have listened in. She does that sometimes."

Pauline went white. "Not to executive calls, I hope?"

Derek shook his head. "She doesn't do the executive switchboard. That's Valerie."

"And does Valerie listen in?"

Derek grinned. "You'll have to ask her."

With Derek gone, Pauline considered her next steps. She'd rattled Fenham with her story; now how could she capitalize on it?

She was still thinking when Ethel Lambton appeared, asking for a few minutes of her "precious" time.

She makes it sound like I haven't long left on this earth, Pauline thought. *Is that a hint?*

"Of course, Ethel. What is it?"

"I've just heard you delivered a report to the boss, naming names. Is that true? Most irregular if it is. The police haven't anyone in custody."

Pauline assured her no names had been mentioned. "The evidence still suggests it may all be mistakes by people confused by the new Rocket Department code."

Ethel brightened. "I'm so glad. We're a happy company with good employees. I'd hate to think anyone had taken advantage of our faith in each other."

"You've never suspected wrongdoing in all your years here?" Pauline asked.

"Never!" Ethel said emphatically.

A little too emphatically, Pauline thought.

She slid two purchase orders across the desk, names and signatures hidden. "You're an electrical engineer, what might these components be used for?"

Ethel studied the pages. "Not our rockets, though similar parts are in the guidance systems."

"What about naval guns?"

"Their targeting systems use similar components, but not from this manufacturer," she replied stiffly.

"What might an ordinary person use them for?"

"An ordinary person would have no use for them at all."

"What about an amateur radio enthusiast?" Pauline pressed.

"Possibly," Ethel admitted reluctantly.

"Anyone else?"

"I can't be expected to guess every application," she said coldly.

Sure now Ethel had an idea and wasn't sharing it, Pauline smiled and shifted the topic. "Are there really rumours about names being named?"

"Oh yes. Quite shocking. People have no respect today.

Everything is coarse, callous, and cynical. We were just discussing it at chapel. These are signs of spiritual decline."

"I agree," Pauline said. "Our vicar said much the same. Something in the news must have triggered it."

"Not new," Ethel insisted. "It's as old as time. Look at the communists and their Sputnik. Symptoms of our malaise."

"It is very bad of them," Pauline said lightly. "I only hope their rockets don't make the weather worse."

Ethel frowned. "You're teasing me, Miss Riddell. Feeling deeply doesn't make me a fool."

Pauline smiled. "I don't think you a fool at all. I'm sorry —I was only trying to lighten things."

Ethel seemed mollified and rose. "Thank you for putting my mind at rest. I knew a sensible woman like you wouldn't be naming names." With a curt nod, she left.

"Now what did she really want?" Pauline muttered. I wonder if Ramsay could get a warrant to search her home. Those components are expensive, and Ethel is an electrical engineer. Who more likely to want them?

Chapter Nineteen

POLICE DETAIN BOTH SUSPECTS

Pauline was sliding the purchase orders back into their file, still puzzling over who might give her a straightforward account of the components' real uses, when her office door banged open.

Brenda charged in, with Violet right behind her.

"They've taken Bob and Fenham away!" they both cried in unison.

Startled, Pauline rose. "Who has?"

"The police," Brenda said breathlessly, planting herself firmly between Violet and Pauline's desk as Violet tried to push past her.

"Inspector Ramsay?" Pauline asked, faintly offended he hadn't phoned or stopped by her office first.

"No!" Violet blurted.

"Uniformed ones," Brenda clarified, again blocking Violet's advance.

"Did they say why?" Pauline asked.

"They want them to 'help with their inquiries,'" Brenda replied.

Violet, denied her moment, stood silently now, watching intently.

Pauline frowned. What new evidence could Ramsay have found to justify hauling in both of the prime suspects?

"You must phone your friend, the Inspector," Violet urged, seizing her chance when Brenda paused for breath. "Bob's a good man -- you know that. The Inspector will listen to you."

"Inspector Ramsay will have a reason for this, Violet. He won't hold Bob long if there's no need to. I'll speak to him later, but not now."

The two women shuffled reluctantly out, whispering to one another. Brenda shut the door with a firmness Pauline couldn't quite interpret -- was she annoyed at Pauline's answer, or signaling Violet not to return? Pauline shrugged it off.

Her thoughts turned back to the elusive question of the components. She needed an independent engineer, someone without an axe to grind. The radio enthusiast theory fit too neatly with Fenham's interests, but why would he involve Bob Wallace at all? Or worse, forge Wallace's name? The possibilities tangled in her mind.

The phone rang, sharp against her thoughts. She picked it up with an exasperated, "Yes?"

"Miss Riddell," came Ramsay's reassuring voice.

Her heart leapt. At last, a breakthrough!

"I wonder if you could join me and Mr. Wallace at his house?"

"Why?" Pauline demanded, suspicion tightening her tone.

"Because Mr. Wallace would like you here," Ramsay said, mild amusement threading through his words. "He feels he'll get a fairer hearing with you present. His solicitor, unfortunately, can't come immediately."

"What are you doing at Bob's house?" Pauline pressed.

"We've had it under observation since the start of the investigation," Ramsay explained. "This morning, we got the warrant. What we saw was enough."

"And Fenham's house too?"

"Yes," Ramsay confirmed.

"You never told me," she snapped.

"I didn't know I had to," he retorted.

"I suppose not." She sighed. "Where am I to come?"

Ten minutes later Pauline was ushered into Bob Wallace's modest terraced house, just north of the factory. A constable led her to the sitting room, where Ramsay and Bob faced each other over a low coffee table piled with magazines.

"Thank you for coming, Miss Riddell," Ramsay greeted her. "Mr. Wallace has an interesting tale for us."

"It's not a tale," Bob growled, glaring. "It's the truth."

Pauline settled into a chair clearly placed for her, taking in the room as she did. Tidy, almost bare. No feminine touches, only sepia photographs of what must be Bob's parents. On the wall hung a framed technical drawing of one of the company's discontinued naval guns. Nostalgia. At either side of the room, two large black boxes stood like sentries. Against the far wall, a wooden console with a record turntable sat in pride of place.

"Go on, Mr. Wallace," Ramsay prompted. A heavy thump from upstairs punctuated his words.

"You'll pay for anything broken," Bob muttered darkly at the ceiling.

"Never mind that," Ramsay replied. He gestured at the console. "Tell us about this."

Bob leaned forward, his eyes lighting as he spoke. "I was in Jeavons, the record shop, last year. They demonstrated a new kind of gramophone, 'high fidelity,' they called it, or hifi. The first record they played sounded like a train rushing through the room. You could hear it pass right by. It was stunning."

"Stunning," Ramsay repeated, sarcastically.

"You weren't there," Wallace retorted. "The second demonstration record was of an orchestra playing, with the strings on one side of the room and brass on the other. It was as if the orchestra was right there in the room with us." Bob's excitement remembering the experience was reflected in his voice.

"I think I'd prefer the train," Ramsay said.

"Obviously, you don't like music, or you'd understand what this meant," Wallace growled.

Pauline glanced at the magazines on the table, *Hi-Fi World*, *Practical Electronics*. A whole other life, quietly pursued under everyone's noses.

"You built this yourself?" she asked, nodding to the console and the looming speakers.

Bob nodded. "I couldn't afford the shop price, not even on hire-purchase. But I realised I could build one, by buying the parts cheaper, piece by piece. So that's what I did."

"With a little help from your company's order books," Ramsay interjected.

Bob's jaw set. "Most of it I bought myself."

"Yet your name appears on purchase orders for parts that we'll find right here," Ramsay pressed.

Bob reddened. "Some were dearer than I could manage at once. If I'd waited, they might have been gone. I thought -- why not get them now, while I saved the money? I was going to pay the company back." His voice cracked. He looked directly at Pauline. "I swear it."

"How soon?" Pauline asked gently.

Bob hesitated. His silence was answer enough.

Ramsay's tone sharpened. "Then we'll also forget your denial of writing those purchase orders?"

Bob nodded, eyes downcast.

"What made you risk your job and your name, Bob?" Pauline asked softly.

"Music," he said simply. "This house has been empty since my parents died. Just me, the wireless, and Bach. When I heard Bach on that hi-fi..." He broke off, then whispered, "It was like hearing him for the first time."

"That's the strangest excuse for theft I've heard," Ramsay said coldly.

"Not theft -- borrowing!" Bob shot back. "A loan. I'd pay it back."

"And when Neville began sniffing around?" Pauline pressed. "You knew he'd find your forged orders sooner or later."

Bob groaned, dropping his head into his hands. "I had nothing to do with Neville's death. Nothing to do with the fire."

A knock at the door cut across his plea. A constable entered with a message. Ramsay rose and stepped outside.

Pauline leaned closer. "This is the moment, Bob. If there's something you want to say—say it now."

He shook his head. "You'd tell them anyway."

Ramsay returned, grim-faced. "Looks like it's you, Bob. You're our man."

"What's Fenham said?" Bob demanded.

"I can't tell you that," Ramsay said smoothly. "Just as I won't tell him what you've said."

"I've not said anything about him!" Bob cried.

"That's the Prisoner's Dilemma, Bob. First man to talk gets the better deal but gains a lifelong enemy."

Panic flared in Bob's eyes. "I helped him with some orders -- yes. But that's all. He was becoming worried because he'd bought too many parts for his own use. He wanted to spread the last few purchases differently, camouflage them, like. I swear I know nothing of the fire."

"You'd say that," Ramsay replied. Then, firmly: "Robert Wallace, I'm arresting you on suspicion of arson, theft, and the deliberate killing of Neville Halliday." He recited the familiar caution as the constable stepped forward.

Bob's shoulders sagged as he was led away.

Pauline exhaled slowly. "Has Fenham told you Bob set the fire?"

"Did I say he had?" Ramsay asked, a glint in his eye.

She frowned. "Then why arrest Bob?"

"There was nothing at Fenham's house. Nothing at all. He still lives with his parents, did you know?"

Pauline shook her head. "Then where's he hiding it?"

"Urmston's checking lockups. He's good at paperwork," Ramsay said.

Pauline gave him a look. "Is that why you got the warrants?"

"Partly. Also because we discovered Wallace started life as an electrician. I'd assumed foremen were mechanical men. Turns out I was wrong."

"And Fenham?"

"Blaming confusion caused by the new Rocket Department codes. Generously offering to shoulder some of the blame."

"How noble," Pauline muttered.

"That leaves Bob the only embezzler with a motive to silence Neville," Ramsay said with finality.

Pauline thought of Bob's bare, lonely house, and his eyes lighting with joy at the memory of Bach. "I'll try to persuade my boss to drop the company prosecution. With a repayment, the matter might be better buried."

"That's your call," Ramsay said. "But I'd hold off. He may yet confess more."

Pauline nodded. But as she walked back to the factory, a whispering crowd already gathering, she wondered uneasily: If Bob wasn't lying, then who was hiding Fenham's loot?

Chapter Twenty

BOTH SUSPECTS RELEASED

The following day began as the previous one had ended: with everyone demanding to know what was happening. From the Managing Director down to the janitors, Pauline faced a steady stream of inquiries.

Her stock reply -- that the police did not keep her as informed as her colleagues imagined, or as much as she would wish, and that she was just as eager for news as they were -- fell flat every time. Few saw the humor, and more than one retorted with suggestions Pauline found hard to stomach. By mid-morning, she felt her relationships with several coworkers were permanently soured. Perhaps, she thought darkly, the company's looming demise would not be such a bad thing after all.

Her boss phoned late morning.

"The police haven't been in touch today?" he demanded.

"Not with me," Pauline replied, allowing a meaningful pause.

"Nor me," he grumbled. "It's our company they're meddling with. You'd think they'd show some sympathy."

"They may have nothing to report," Pauline reminded him. "If Bob doesn't confess to the fire, then they've no serious charge. A public prosecution might do us more harm than good."

It felt like the right moment to introduce her idea. "Perhaps we should consider dropping the charges."

"Stealing is a serious crime, Pauline."

"Of course," she agreed smoothly. "And he can't continue here, even if he isn't charged. Only, people may see it as unfair. Last month we let two pipefitters go for stealing scrap. We didn't involve the police."

Her boss huffed that those cases were 'entirely different,' and he concluded by asking her to call the instant she heard anything. Pauline hung up with a small, satisfied smile. She'd planted doubt in his mind -- doubt she could build on if, as seemed likely, Bob continued to deny arson and Neville's death.

Fenham, she noted, was back at work. She half-expected him to appear at her office, smirking at her failure to prove his guilt. He did not. Edith, too, stayed away. The silence was unnerving. Even the canteen was hushed at lunchtime. The whole office seemed to be holding its breath -- or perhaps avoiding her, resentful that she had supplied the police with evidence.

She convened her small team in the afternoon.

"There's nothing older than a year," Fred reported. "We've got everything from then to now."

"Maybe it was just the new Rocket Department code," Pauline mused. "Poorly thought out, leading to mistakes."

Ian shook his head. "No. That code was almost certainly Fenham's idea. He knew exactly how badly it would be implemented. I think the 'mistakes' were intentional."

"Can we prove it?" Pauline asked.

"If we could find the minutes of the coding meetings," Ian said.

"They'll be in Purchasing," Pauline replied. "Not in a general vault. Brenda?"

"Important documents go to the company library," Brenda said, "but these probably weren't considered important enough."

"They should have been," Fred countered. "If everyone's to use these codes, they belong there. At least the staff memo will be."

Pauline nodded. "Brenda, track that down. I'll ask Derek if he has a copy—he was Neville's deputy. The MD's office might hold one too."

"I'll search Purchasing's vault," Ian volunteered. His colleagues agreed to help.

"We'll meet at day's end," Pauline decided.

Derek, when she found him, proved unhelpful. His desk and all his documents had gone up in flames.

"I do remember a memo," he admitted. "Told us what code to use. That's all. I'd never seen a purchasing code before, so it didn't look odd to me."

Pauline returned to her office discouraged, only to find Brenda waiting with a mimeographed copy of the memo itself.

"Thank you, Brenda," Pauline said, brightening. "Anything with it?"

"Nothing. Just this."

The memo laid out the codes for the Rocket Department and its subsections—electrical, mechanical, fuel, and more. Suggestive, but hardly incriminating.

Later, over tea and a digestive biscuit, Pauline tried to console herself with small comforts. But by the time her team reconvened, she knew the day would end in disappointment.

"Nothing," Ian reported flatly. "We need access to Purchasing's files. Call Fenham. If he refuses, we'll know he's hiding something."

"And tip him off to destroy it?" Pauline countered.

"Then we burgle it tonight," Ian said with a grin.

"No," Pauline said firmly. "Let the matter rest for now. We'll wait. If Bob is innocent, he may yet point the finger at Fenham."

Her team left reluctantly. If their inquiries hadn't alerted Fenham, she thought she might do her own spot of burgling after hours.

By late afternoon the staff streamed out into the October rain. Pauline lingered, watching them from her window. At last, with the building nearly silent, she slipped down the corridor to the Purchasing offices.

The door yielded easily. Inside, only security lights glowed, throwing long shadows over empty desks. Fenham's secretary had left her lamp on, a lonely pool of light on the blotter.

Pauline's eyes went instead to the filing cabinet. Locked, of course. But the company's cabinets were notoriously uniform. Almost any key opened almost any drawer. Hers did.

The code file was nearly a year old, tucked into a lower drawer. Heart pounding, Pauline leafed through until she found the minutes.

One manager had objected to the code, warning it would confuse staff. Fenham had agreed, then argued it preserved the company's structure and required less retraining. He promised the Rocket Department would be well trained and closely supervised. The code had been approved.

Pauline hesitated, then slid the file into her bag. Evidence -- circumstantial, but damning -- that Fenham had designed and pushed through a flawed system.

Back in her office, she copied the pages, hiding them among her staffing files where Brenda would not stumble on them. Returning the originals could wait.

The phone shrilled, startling her. A black thought struck -- had someone seen her in Purchasing? Was this blackmail? She forced herself to answer briskly.

"Yes?"

"He has an alibi," Ramsay said without preamble.

"Bob?" Pauline asked, astonished. "I thought he lived alone?"

"He does," Ramsay chuckled. "But across the street lives a widow with a sharp eye. She's kept chapter and verse on his movements for a month. One of my constables spoke to her."

"She's sure?"

"I've just been myself," Ramsay said, amusement in his voice. "She knows everything about everyone. And she thinks Bob is a 'nice man.'"

"She might be angling for a marriage proposal," Pauline suggested, laughing.

"Possible," Ramsay conceded. "But when I told her about Halliday's death, she didn't flinch. I believe her."

Relief swept through Pauline.

"But that's not the only reason I called," Ramsay added. "Mr. Wallace insists you're his guardian angel. He wants you present for another chat."

144

"Not tonight," Pauline said wearily. "I'm too tired to hear Bob justify why robbery is acceptable when he does it."

Ramsay laughed. "Fair enough. Tomorrow then. My office, after lunch?"

They agreed on a time and hung up.

Pauline sat staring at the receiver. What more can this 'nice man' possibly have to say? she wondered. Too late, she regretted not going at once. Now she'd lie awake, worrying about it all night.

Chapter Twenty-One

HUNTING THE RUNAWAY

In Ramsay's office, arms folded, Bob sat across the desk from Pauline and Ramsay, his expression stony. Far from wanting to talk, he now seemed determined to say nothing.

"Look, Bob," Pauline said, "we want to help you. The police have evidence clearing you of the fire, so we know you weren't in any way responsible for Neville's death. Helping Fenham with some small thefts isn't going to send you to prison for life. But someone set the conditions just right for that fire. Fenham's the villain here, not you."

"Then question *him*," Bob said.

Pauline shook her head. "We can't. When he left work last night, he didn't go home, and he isn't in work today. He phoned to say he needed time off because of the stress the police had put him under."

"I can believe he does," Bob replied, glaring at Ramsay.

"He didn't say where, and his parents are refusing to help us," Ramsay told him. "They're also upset at the events of the past week."

"They can join the queue," Bob said. "It's been a nightmare."

"By your own admission, Mr. Wallace," Ramsay told him, "you are a thief. Your 'nightmare' is your own doing."

Bob's expression grew sullen at this rebuke and Pauline jumped in to smooth the waters. "Maybe you can tell us where to find him. Your assistance in bringing a murderer to justice will go a long way in how people think of you in the future."

He stared at her, and for some time it seemed he wasn't going to speak. The silence grew, and Ramsay added, "What Miss Riddell says is true, Mr. Wallace. You're in a pickle but not so bad you can't escape. Do the right thing, and we'll do right by you."

Bob's gaze turned to him as if judging how much confidence he should place in a policeman. Finally, he said, "When my lawyer is here, I'll tell you what you want to know. I want a witness on my side."

Ramsay nodded. "Very well, we'll wait." He signaled the hovering constable to take Bob away. "Whichever interview room is free," Ramsay told him.

When the two were gone, Pauline said, "I'd hoped he would tell us without making it all legal and official."

Ramsay nodded. "It would have been nice, but I understand his wanting a supporter to hear it. He has no reason to believe we would choose to remember what he'd done when all this comes to court."

He'd barely finished speaking when the desk sergeant poked his head around the door to announce the arrival of Mr. Wallace's solicitor.

"Good," Ramsay cried, rising from his chair. "We can get started." He turned to Pauline. "I'm afraid you can't be present, Miss Riddell. Will you wait, or should I phone you when we have Fenham's bolthole?"

"I'll wait. I think he's made his mind up to tell us," Pauline replied.

Ramsay settled himself in the seat opposite Wallace and asked, "Well?"

It was the lawyer who spoke first. "I've advised my client to assist you in any way he can, Inspector. However, I'm advising him now not to respond to a general search for information such as you asking 'well?' We will answer questions pertinent to the case and no more."

Ramsay rolled his eyes but asked, in a neutral tone, "Can you tell me where we might find Mr. Fenham? We would like to interview him in relation to our enquiries concerning fraudulent use of a company's purchasing system."

Bob nodded. "He told me, years ago, he'd bought an abandoned farm worker's cottage out Kielder way."

"Can you be more precise?" Ramsay asked.

"Not exactly," Bob admitted. "I never went there nor talked to him about it. He was getting into astronomy, had a telescope and the like. He said you could hardly see the moon through the skies over Newcastle, there's that much soot in the air."

Ramsay smiled. "I'm sure he's right. Some days, just blowing my nose leaves my handkerchief black."

"He said the cottage had clear skies above, no soot from the west, and a perfect view north," Bob continued.

Ramsay had never been so far out into the hinterland of Northumberland, but he imagined it might be the place for stargazing. After all, no one lived there apart from lonely farms and thousands of sheep.

"Anything else?" he asked.

"There are no neighbors, it's off an unnumbered road, and there's a clear stream at the bottom of the garden," Bob added. "Fenham said, if the lunatics who govern us all do blow up the planet, he'll be able to live up there forever without any difficulty."

"And yet you never visited," Ramsay responded wryly.

Bob grinned. "I'm a city boy myself."

"How did you come to fall in with Fenham and his mad scheme?" Ramsay asked.

"They say, 'my enemy's enemy is my friend,' don't they?" Bob answered. "When I saw Violet going out with Fenham, I was upset. He's not the right man for her," he paused, "or any woman, I'd say. Nasty feel about him for all his soft ways."

"But when Neville stepped in?" Ramsay prompted.

Bob nodded unhappily. "I never really knew how much I loved her -- or even that I loved her as a man loves a woman -- until she started seeing Neville. The boys she'd gone out with, and then Fenham, none of them bothered me too much, but Neville was a serious young man who was going places."

"And you were jealous," Ramsay said, as it didn't seem that Wallace would be able to say it.

Bob nodded. "Like I said. I didn't know myself until then. All these years watching her, thinking I felt fondly toward her, brotherly or fatherly-like…"

"So, when Fenham suggested killing Neville…" Ramsay began.

"No!" Bob almost shouted. "Fenham said he had a scheme to get him fired, nothing else."

"Why did he tell you?" Ramsay asked.

Bob's expression spoke of terrible internal conflict, as he said, "I made the mistake of criticizing Neville's behavior toward Violet, and he saw the opportunity. He presented the idea as a joke at first."

"Then, when he saw you jump at it, he made it real?" Ramsay asked.

Nodding, Bob continued, "He needed me on the inside to make it work. As a foreman in the Rocket Department, I could be there when shipments arrived and create purchase orders with Neville's name on them."

"And Fenham in Purchasing could slide them all through without anyone asking questions," Ramsay added.

"We were preparing to spring the trap, hand over our evidence of corruption in the Rocket Department," Bob said, "when the place burned down, and Neville was killed. That was an accident. Nothing to do with us."

"Well, nothing to do with you maybe," Ramsay agreed, "but you still thought you'd better clean up any incriminating paperwork."

Bob nodded miserably. "With Neville's death, there'd be a serious inquiry and the nonsensical petty purchases we'd made to make Neville look like a crook would be investigated. I had to find the paperwork and destroy it."

"Unfortunately for you, Neville had already started the investigation before he died," Ramsay said. "It was unraveling, and he had to be silenced. Isn't that what happened?"

"Not by me," Bob replied emphatically. "And I don't believe Fenham did it either. It must have been an accident. Just bad luck for all of us."

Ramsay frowned. One of the hardest parts of an investigator's job was getting a feel for the person being interviewed, trying to decide what was simple denial and what was honesty. Despite his scepticism, he felt Wallace was telling the truth.

"The thing is, Bob," Ramsay said, "I can't believe in the coincidence of Neville dying just as he was bringing your embezzlement out into the open. It's too convenient. I'm sure you can see that?"

"Not for me, it isn't," Bob cried. "It's a nightmare."

"Then maybe you should just tell us what Fenham did that night and help us to see your innocence?"

"I'm telling you I wasn't there that night, and so far as I know, Fenham wasn't either," Bob responded.

"Why do you say that? Surely you know, or you don't?" Ramsay asked.

"When we met the next morning, we both asked, 'what happened?' I'm sure he was as in the dark as I was," Bob answered.

"That's your evidence for believing him innocent?" Ramsay asked.

"I believed him then; I still do. He was stunned by Neville's death and the destruction of the rocket shed. Nothing like that was supposed to happen."

"Maybe it was someone else?" Ramsay asked. "Who else was in your plot?"

"Nobody," Bob said. "Why won't you believe me? It was an accident."

"Because of the timing and because Neville was not a shoddy workman," Ramsay replied. "Have you anything to say that would be more convincing?"

Bob shook his head.

"Then I'm going to ask you to read and sign your statement taken by my constable here," he pointed to the note-taker sitting against the wall. "He will quickly type it up and then you can go. But don't go far. We would find that very suspicious."

Ramsay left the interview room and went to find Pauline, who was waiting patiently in his office.

"Well?" she asked.

"We need a map of the Kielder area," Ramsay told her. "With luck, and some map reading, I think we can be soon on our way."

It wasn't as quick as Ramsay had hoped, but they found two possible locations that fitted Wallace's description of the cottage.

And when they drove out to Kielder, they found the first was still derelict, but the second had smoke rising from its chimney and the air of a cottage in use.

Chapter Twenty-Two

THE VILLAIN'S LAIR

Fenham's cottage may once have been the farmworker's dwelling Bob had described, but that was years ago. Now it was a robust, two-storey building with a newly slated roof surrounding a strange round turret capped by a glass dome.

"He's a stargazer," Ramsay whispered, as they surveyed the building from across the dale. "That's an observatory."

"Which may explain some of the radio components he's been buying," Pauline said. "Maybe he's in contact with other astronomers around the world."

Ramsay grimaced. "You don't think we've stumbled on another nest of Soviet spies, do you?"

Pauline considered this. "I don't think he would make it all so obvious if he was."

"On the contrary," Ramsay replied. "If his cover is that he's an astronomer, I think he'd be as obvious as he could be."

"Our office workers are scrutinized by the security services, you know," Pauline countered. "They want to be sure our military secrets don't fall into foreign hands. This must have been investigated by them, I imagine."

"Again, I say, it's a brilliant cover for a spy," Ramsay said.

Pauline nodded. What the Inspector said was true -- yet she hoped it wasn't. Still, a remote cottage, an observatory, and unexplained radio components were powerful reasons for doubt.

"If he is," Pauline said quietly, "he may be armed. Shouldn't we call for some armed police to assist? Walking in there thinking we're accusing him of petty theft only to find he's a fully trained Moscow agent would be a bad mistake."

Ramsay considered. It was a long way back to the main road and a phone box. And having a fully armed team turn up at the private residence of an innocent amateur astronomer and radio 'ham' would be excruciatingly embarrassing.

"You stay here, well away from the cottage," he said at last. "I'll go and scout out the situation. If I think there's a need for armed support, I'll return, and we'll go for help."

Pauline studied the cottage through her binoculars. "I can see him in the upper floor window," she said. "He seems to be working on something. Maybe the radio?"

"It's certainly too early for the telescope," Ramsay agreed, "being just after midday. I'm going on foot. You stay! That's an order."

Pauline gave him an ironic 'yes, sir' and watched him stride away down the valley side, keeping among the gorse and broom wherever he could. Soon he'd crossed the narrow stream at the bottom of the valley and began making his way up toward the cottage. Again, Ramsay made full use of the cover provided by stone walls, hedges, and gorse. Finally, he reached the cottage and disappeared. Pauline imagined he'd gone to the back of the building to investigate there.

She checked her watch, noting the time he'd disappeared. Minutes later, when he hadn't re-appeared, she looked again. Only five minutes had passed -- barely enough time to look through the ground-floor windows, let alone search the outbuildings.

When she became truly uneasy, Pauline looked again. Twenty minutes now, and still no sign of Ramsay. She set off in pursuit. If he was in trouble, she needed to know before raising an alarm.

The climb down the valley side was more difficult than she'd expected, but soon she was leaping across the stream -- swollen with overnight rain -- and creeping as carefully as she could up the hillside. As she did, she suddenly realized that while the telescope might not be useful for stargazing at midday, it would be perfect for identifying a car and its occupants watching the house from across the valley. Had Ramsay walked into a trap? And was she walking into the same trap?

Pauline waited in the lee of a hawthorn bush, bent and twisted by decades of the prevailing wind sweeping down the narrow valley from the west. There was no sign of life at the cottage beyond the smoke lazily rising from the chimney before being dissipated by the breeze. She started cautiously moving toward the building, watching for movement at the windows or doors. There was none.

Around the back of the building, she'd hoped to find Ramsay examining something so important it had taken nearly thirty minutes to digest. He wasn't anywhere in sight. She crept forward, peeking into the two partly open doors of the outbuildings. One held Fenham's car. The other was empty, which meant Ramsay must be inside confronting Fenham -- though why she couldn't hear their voices was a mystery.

After making sure she wouldn't be seen, Pauline ran lightly across the cobbled yard to the cottage, pressing herself against the wall near the door. No sounds came from inside. She decided the thick stone walls must be muffling everything. For all she knew, a desperate struggle was going on inside and Ramsay needed her help. The thought made her smile. Ramsay may be the older of the two men, but she couldn't see Fenham easily overcoming him.

Pauline turned the handle on the door and found it unlocked. Quietly, she eased it open until she could see into the kitchen. No one was there. Stepping inside, she closed the door behind her. The hinges squeaked. The sound was as quiet as mice, but in her heightened excitement it seemed like elephants trumpeting.

The kitchen floor was flagstone, and Pauline crossed it silently to the step up to the next level, where she stopped. This floor was newly laid wood, and she knew her shoes would squeak on the polish and the planks would creak under her weight. Slipping her shoes off, she carefully crossed to the stairs. These too looked new and polished.

As she debated her next move, she heard Fenham talking above her head. Was he speaking to Ramsay -- or someone else? There was no other car parked around the house, so it could only be Ramsay. With a sigh of relief, she slipped her shoes back on and mounted the stairs. As she ascended, Fenham's voice became clearer. He was speaking to someone who wasn't replying.

The mystery was solved when she reached the landing and saw Fenham through the gap of a partly open door.

He had his back to her and was wearing large headphones of the sort you saw in movies. No doubt bought with company money, Pauline thought indignantly. But where was Ramsay?

Fenham continued talking, speaking slowly as though the person listening wasn't fluent in English. That explained it -- he was on longwave radio, speaking to someone in a foreign country.

Pauline's heart sank. Was this about spying after all? Her very first experience of murder came back vividly, and anger instantly consumed her. How could he do this? It was one thing to be a criminal, but a traitor was immeasurably worse.

Chapter Twenty-Three

CONFRONTATION

Pushing open the door, Pauline strode into the room, startling Fenham. He wrenched around in his chair, saw her, flung off the headset, and leapt to his feet.

"You," he growled. "With your lapdog Ramsay?"

"It's no good, Morris," Pauline replied, standing her ground as he advanced, fists clenched, face contorted with fury. Despite his rage, she didn't see him as truly dangerous. Life had made him sly, not violent. "Inspector Ramsay is here. You can't get away by killing me as well."

She'd guessed right. He stopped dead, only an arm's length away.

"I've killed no one," he cried. "No one!"

"Neville was an accident?" Pauline pressed, certain she now had the upper hand.

"I didn't start the fire," Fenham said, sullen now. "That was him -- careless, with no regard for anyone or anything. Not even his own safety."

"He never struck me as careless," Pauline retorted. "Or disregarding others. Was it just you he disregarded?"

158

That struck a nerve. He lunged forward, hands grabbing at her throat. Pauline had grown overconfident, and his thumbs pressed into her windpipe before she could react. She tried to bring her knee up between his thighs, but he twisted, and her knee struck only his leg. His grip tightened, crushing her throat and cutting off her breath. Desperate, Pauline scratched at his eyes, but his head jerked too much for her nails to do real damage.

Suddenly, behind Fenham's head she saw Ramsay -- his fist raised, baton in hand. It came down with a sickening thud. Fenham staggered, went limp, then a second blow sent him sprawling to the floor.

"Are you all right, Miss Riddell?" Ramsay asked, concern etched on his face.

Pauline gulped, decided her throat was fine, and managed, "Right as rain, Inspector. Where were you?"

"In that side room," he said, pointing. "I was hoping to hear something incriminating. I hadn't quite given up on my spy theory, you see."

"I think we spend too much time thinking and talking about spies," Pauline said crossly. "I blame it on television."

"And modern books," Ramsay replied, as he handcuffed the unconscious Fenham. "And the radio. And the newspapers."

Pauline laughed. "Well, you must admit they do go on a bit. Fenham's just a radio 'ham,' isn't he?"

"Afraid so," Ramsay said with a grin. "At least on this occasion, he was. I know the weather in Kuala Lumpur, if you're interested."

"That's who he was speaking to?" Pauline asked. "I guessed it was someone for whom English wasn't their first language."

Fenham groaned and tried to sit up. Ramsay hauled

him to his feet and marched him toward the door. Pauline followed. At the radio set, she flicked off the power switch. "We don't want this place burning down too," she said.

Ramsay nodded. "There's plenty of evidence in here," he agreed, pushing Fenham ahead of him.

On the stairs, Fenham muttered, "I can pay the company back for everything. They've no reason to press charges. Your assault on me will haunt you, Inspector."

"I stopped you murdering Miss Riddell," Ramsay replied calmly.

"It's her word against mine," Fenham sneered. "I say you two attacked me and I defended myself."

"You're a wanted man, Mr. Fenham," Ramsay said. "The bruises on Miss Riddell's throat will speak louder than either of us."

"Wanted for what?" Fenham scoffed as they exited the cottage. "Some small embezzlement? That doesn't warrant assault."

"Give it a rest," Ramsay told him, steering him down the slope toward the police car across the valley.

Pauline asked, "Is your telescope just for stargazing, Morris? Or is it Sputnik you're watching? Does it give you orders?"

Fenham laughed. "You read too many trashy novels, Miss Riddell. That's ridiculous."

"Will a judge think so?" Ramsay wondered aloud, helping Fenham up the bank. "Would a jury believe Sputnik had no purpose, and that you -- with your telescope and radio -- just happened to be here watching the stars when it was launched?"

"You think the Russians launched the world's first satellite just to talk to me? Are you mad?" Fenham shouted.

"Maybe it isn't just you," Pauline said. "Maybe there are dozens like you, scattered across the West."

"Mad!" Fenham barked, shaking his head.

His words sounded confident, but Pauline sensed his doubt. "Even if it is mad," she said, as Ramsay bundled him into the car, "people believe stranger things. And on top of murder, arson, and theft, it makes a strong impression against you."

Ramsay handed her the keys.

"You drive," he said. "I'll sit in the back to keep him in line."

Back at the police station, Pauline watched Fenham led inside while Ramsay stayed back. She knew what he was about to say but still bristled.

"We'll take over from here, Miss Riddell," Ramsay told her. "It's a police matter now."

"Of course," Pauline said, though aggrieved. "Still, you'd get on better if I were there. He and I know each other, and while I can't pretend we're friends, I'd get more from him talking naturally than you will in an interview."

Ramsay laughed. "That's true of every case. There's always someone who'd get more, but we can't allow it. The transcript would be useless in court."

Pauline smiled faintly. It was true, though it didn't ease her frustration. "You will let me know what comes from this, won't you?"

"When I can," Ramsay replied guardedly. "Trust me, Miss Riddell, I value your help — and you coming to my assistance earlier, even if I wasn't in danger. But in the end, I'm a police officer. I have to follow the rules."

"As long as we get a conviction for Neville's death, whether manslaughter or murder, I'll be satisfied," Pauline said.

"You're not swayed by his protests of innocence?" Ramsay asked.

"I'm not," she answered. "What you told me of Bob's testimony convinces me it was Fenham."

"Not an accident?" Ramsay pressed.

"A fortuitous accident?" Pauline grimaced. "Possible, but I think not. Why? Are you coming around to the idea he's innocent?"

Ramsay laughed. "I follow the evidence. My opinions come second." With a smile, he bade her goodbye and turned to follow Fenham inside. At the entrance, he stopped and called back: "What am I thinking? Miss Riddell, the police doctor needs to examine your injuries. Come along."

The doctor was already tending Fenham's head wound when they arrived. Pauline had to wait, muttering, "My bruises will be gone before he even sees me." She checked her watch. If the doctor was quick, there was still time to get back to the office before everyone left.

At last, she was examined and released. Refusing a police car, she reasoned it would only fuel gossip if she arrived at work that way.

Catching a bus at the Haymarket, Pauline returned to the office. The gate guard gave her a puzzled look as she showed her card.

"You're right," she told him. "After all I've done for the police, they could have given me a lift back here."

He grinned and waved her through.

At the Managing Director's office, she was fortunate to find him alone. After recounting her day, and its implications for the company, he frowned. "Never mind that. Get down to the medical office and have those bruises recorded. The police should have done that."

"They did -- or I'd have been here an hour ago," Pauline said. "Really, I'm fine. He hadn't time to get a good grip."

Her boss grimaced. "Fortunately for you and us. Did he kill Neville Halliday?"

"I think so," Pauline said, then added, "I hope so. If it was an accident from poor practices, we'll have safety inspectors crawling over us for years."

He nodded. "I hate to say it, but I agree. From our point of view, Fenham as the perpetrator gives us breathing space. The company is struggling."

"Then give Derek Parker the Rocket Department," Pauline urged. "Luke Morgan will snuff it out."

The MD shook his head. "Neville was young, but he could manage men. Parker, for all his talents, can't."

That didn't surprise Pauline. Derek never pushed himself forward; he waited to be asked.

"Then find someone from outside," she said. "Someone who lives and breathes rockets."

He nodded reluctantly. "That's what we should do. But the founder's family still controls this company, and they aren't interested in rockets."

This news crushed Pauline. Without a new product line, the company's future was bleak. She might soon need to find work elsewhere. But jobs were vanishing — ship-building and everything tied to it was fading. Could she stay in Newcastle, the city she'd grown to love?

Leaving the MD's office, she gloomily returned to her own. She reached for the phone to call Ramsay, then put it down. He'd call when he had news. Still restless, she went home.

After dinner, washing up, and a futile attempt at reading, the phone finally rang. She snatched it up.

"Yes?"

"We should meet," Ramsay said.

Chapter Twenty-Four

A KILLER UNMASKED

"He's still saying he had nothing to do with the fire or Neville's death," Ramsay told Pauline.

They were sitting once again in the snug of the *Seven Stars*. It was a rundown, weary pub at the end of its natural life. Its regulars had long since moved away, and it now survived on people returning to their old 'local' out of habit, or those driving out of town for a quiet evening. Few came for the food, and Ramsay and Pauline stuck to drinks in the quiet snug, where they were invariably alone.

Pauline frowned. "It has always bothered me that he wouldn't know how to create that 'cocktail of chemicals' the safety report described. The only two people I think could do that are Bob Wallace and Ethel Lambton."

"My money's on Bob," Ramsay replied. "He helped Fenham when he thought Fenham was just trying to have Neville fired. He said he stopped when Neville was killed. However, it's also possible he stopped when he used Fenham's strategy to remove Neville as a rival."

"And maybe he planned to remove Fenham next, but we

got involved," Pauline added. Her heart sank as she spoke. She liked Bob, and she'd been devastated when she learned he'd helped Fenham at all.

Ramsay agreed. "He was also the most familiar with the Rocket Club and its building, equipment, and stores."

"Ethel was close too, and her education is stronger than Bob's," Pauline argued. "She's my pick, only I don't see how we prove it."

"We get one of our two culprits to talk," Ramsay replied. "My next step is going to be offering Fenham a deal. He says it wasn't him who frayed the cable that led to Neville's death. I'll suggest he tell me who did, and we won't charge him with the murder."

"He won't accept because you haven't been able to provide evidence he did," Pauline countered.

Ramsay nodded. "Until now, I've expected him to confess. After all, we were only talking of manslaughter then."

"What has changed now?" Pauline asked.

"Now I believe him," Ramsay said. "His stubbornness over being innocent of the fire and Neville's death has convinced me. I've interviewed hundreds of people proclaiming their innocence, and I assumed he was just another of that kind."

"Now you think he's different?"

Ramsay's expression remained serious. "I do. And I think he's shielding someone. That most likely 'someone' is Violet."

Pauline considered this carefully. "Then use Violet as the lever. If he thinks you're going after the person he's shielding, he may give us Ethel, which is my first choice."

Ramsay shook his head. "Why didn't he point to Ethel right away? Why would he only mention her when he must know I'll likely take that to mean it was really Violet or Wallace?"

"Either way," Pauline said, "we'll learn something new."

"I hope so," Ramsay replied, "because we have no other means of getting the evidence we need."

Pauline shrugged. "Do it. Sooner the better."

Ramsay grinned. "I intend to. My trip out this evening to meet with you is just me letting him stew in a cell so the new approach will hit him harder."

"You're going straight back tonight?" Pauline asked.

"I am. He'll be tired and at a low point. It's rotten, but sometimes we must do these things to get to the truth," Ramsay agreed.

"What if Ethel runs during the night?" Pauline asked.

Ramsay laughed. "I like the way you assume you're right. To answer your objection, it will be long past most people's bedtime, and Fenham won't be warning anyone any time soon, whoever it is."

"If it works, we should know by morning," Pauline said. "You'll phone me the moment you know? I want to watch them at work tomorrow so they can't get away before you arrive to arrest them."

Ramsay smiled. "They won't be at work when he gives me one of them, but I will phone you. Don't shout at me when it's the wee small hours of the morning."

Pauline grinned. "I can't promise, but I'll try."

It was dark and stormy when they left the pub. A stiff breeze blew in from the sea, carrying the smell of seaweed and the less pleasant tang of industrial waste drifting across from cities that ringed the North Sea. A sudden squall lashed them with rain as they wished each other good night. *A foul night for foul deeds*, Pauline thought as she jumped into her car and slammed the door shut.

The call she'd been waiting for, while staring silently at her bedroom ceiling lit occasionally by lightning flashes, came just after one o'clock in the morning.

"You were right," Ramsay told her. "It was Ethel. I have two constables on their way to her house right now. I'm sorry it was her. She's been a great help to her parents and many others in the chapel's congregation. She'll be sadly missed by many older people."

Pauline found herself unable to sleep after this and went into the kitchen to make a cup of tea. She had barely picked up the electric kettle when the phone rang again. Hurrying back to the hall, Pauline snatched up the handset. "Yes?"

"She's gone," Ramsay told her. "Her parents say she's on vacation in Yorkshire. Didn't you notice her missing at work?"

"We don't really meet often at work," Pauline admitted. "Where in Yorkshire? My family are down there, maybe they could find her?"

"The police will find her," Ramsay said. "It's only a matter of time."

"They should be quick then," Pauline retorted. "People like Ethel have strong feelings about crime and punishment. I suspect we may already be too late."

Ramsay was quiet for a moment. "And I fear you may be right. She left two days ago, her parents said. I guess she'd already decided Fenham would betray her."

"Why didn't he say all this days ago?" Pauline cried. "What was Ethel to him?"

Ramsay sighed. "As I mentioned, she did a lot of charitable work among the elderly, and Fenham's parents were among those she helped. She and Fenham had become close, you see."

Pauline's insides were doing acrobatics, and she felt ill. "We must hope for the best. A judge may be lenient, and she may still have a future life after her sentence is served."

"The chemical cocktail was meant to kill," Ramsay reminded her. "And wanting revenge on someone for getting a position she wanted isn't a 'crime of passion' that anyone might look kindly upon."

Pauline couldn't argue. "Then it's best if she's punished herself. Suicide will be much less painful for her family and friends."

"They won't see it that way," Ramsay said. "Because if she has, we won't share the details of Neville's death. They won't know the worse alternative she faced."

"I'm not going to be able to sleep now," Pauline told him. "But thank you for letting me know."

Ramsay rang off, and Pauline returned to the kitchen.

Work that day was painful. Everything went on as it usually did. No one knew what Pauline knew, and occasionally their words stabbed her with their insensitivity. She kept the knowledge to herself. It made it easier to discover where people thought Ethel was. Some said West Yorkshire, some remembered her saying East Yorkshire, others thought she had said she was going abroad. This last gave Pauline a shadow of hope. She'd liked Neville but hadn't known him. He was dead and couldn't be brought back. Executing his murderer hardly seemed a priority now.

No one could say for sure where Ethel was, and that too was a relief. Pauline didn't want to be the one telling the police where Ethel might be found, though she knew she would if she learned.

By late afternoon, she couldn't wait any longer and phoned Ramsay. "Have you found her?" she demanded, when he was brought to the phone.

"I'll phone you the moment I hear anything," he replied. "You'll be the first to know."

Understanding that he meant her not to phone him again, Pauline thanked him and rang off.

Her surprise that day was having Bob Wallace shuffle into her office at the end of his shift.

"I came to apologise," he said, standing inside the door. "I should have told you about my part in Fenham's plot to remove Neville from the company and Violet's life."

Pauline motioned him to a seat, and he took it.

"What were you thinking of?" she asked, though she was sure she knew.

He coloured and fiddled with the cloth cap in his hands. "I was thinking that after Fenham drove Neville out of the company, I could use what Fenham did to separate Violet from him. I had the proof, you see." He looked at her as though she must understand.

"But Bob," Pauline replied, "Violet would hate you for your part in Neville's disgrace as much as she would hate Fenham. Even if you were able to hide your part in it, Fenham wouldn't."

His expression was a mix of shame and misery as he answered, "I'd thought of a clever way to tell Violet. A way that Fenham wouldn't realise it was me that ratted on him."

"You must be very much in love to be this confused, Bob," Pauline said.

He nodded. "I've loved her since she was a girl. I never thought a man as old as me would have a chance with someone as young as Violet. She was so bright and energetic. Then she took up with Fenham."

"And you thought, if she likes him, why not me?" Pauline suggested, and the old George Formby song sprang into her head -- '*If women like them, like men like them, why don't women like me?*'

He nodded again. "Now it's a mess. She was beginning to see me differently when I was ferrying her to work and back, and now she's shocked to find I was in league with Fenham. She says she'll never speak to me again."

Pauline didn't know what to say. Her own feelings toward him were also mixed after learning he was part of Fenham's plot. "They say time heals all. Maybe it will on this occasion."

He shook his head. "How could I ever look her in the face again after what I did? I can barely look at *myself* in the mirror, I'm that ashamed."

Though she sympathised, Pauline couldn't help feeling that was exactly how he should feel. "What are you going to do? You will find it hard to continue working here as the story gets out."

"I've handed in my notice," he replied. "I only came by to say sorry and goodbye."

"You don't need to apologise," Pauline said. "You weren't under any obligation to be honest with me. I should have realised something was wrong when you were able to walk in and out of the Purchasing vault even though you didn't work there."

"I was removing documents even as you were searching for them," he admitted. "By then I was scared I was going to be caught up in Fenham's downfall, which, of course, in the end I was."

"Have you spoken to Violet?"

He nodded. "I tried to explain, but she became upset, and I thought it best to remove myself. Maybe, one day she'll be willing to listen." He paused, then added, "I should leave it for now. 'Least said, soonest mended.' Isn't that how the saying goes?"

Pauline agreed it was, and wished him all the best as she escorted him to the door. She and Brenda watched him go in silence.

"Was he really in with it?" Brenda asked.

Pauline nodded. "I'm afraid so. What fools we become when we fall in love." She wondered if that wasn't true of her. Stephen had been dead four years now. It couldn't hurt him or his parents if she found another man. A sharp pain in her heart told her it would still hurt her. *Fools indeed*, she thought bitterly.

Pauline's anxiety kept her on edge all day and through another long, restless night. Ramsay's phone call, when it came, came the following day.

Chapter Twenty-Five

THE CALM AFTER THE STORM

"You found her?" Pauline cried when she heard Ramsay's greeting. All morning, she'd hovered near her desk waiting for this call. By now, she felt her spirits could only get better, no matter what he said.

"We found her body, yes," Ramsay said. "As we suspected, she punished herself for what she'd done."

"How?" Pauline demanded.

"Horribly," Ramsay replied. "A cocktail of common household cleaning products. She was at least consistent in her choice of weapon."

"Did she leave a note?"

"Two. One for her parents and one for the police," Ramsay said.

"What did she say?" Pauline pressed. It felt like she was pulling teeth; his replies were so lacking in detail.

"To us?" Ramsay replied. "Only that we should say sorry to Neville's parents. She'd acted in a fit of rage she couldn't control." He paused. "I'd say a lifetime of repressed hope finally exploded and, sadly, killed the man who'd done his best for her."

"Isn't that often the way of it," Pauline remarked. "The innocent suffers and the guilty go free?"

"Sadly, it is," Ramsay agreed. "We do our best, but life isn't fair. Not for any of us. Some are hurt more than others."

"I wasn't commenting on the police or the justice system," Pauline responded. "It was more of a thought from the Bible. An eternal verity, if you like."

"It's true of both," Ramsay replied. "Anyway, apart from the trials of Morris Fenham and Bob Wallace for little more than petty larceny, which will end in fines or a short time in prison for one or both of them, this case is over."

"The trials are going ahead, then?" Pauline asked.

"It seems so," Ramsay said. "Your boss is still demanding it."

"A waste of resources, you thought once," Pauline reminded him.

"In many ways, it is," Ramsay told her. "But hiding inside this trail of petty theft was the opportunity for murder, and Ethel Lambton took it. I imagine Fenham guessed, but as long as we told no one about the chemical-soaked cloth, he couldn't be sure she was guilty. Maybe we must treat even small crimes seriously to prevent people graduating to larger ones."

"You sound like one of those people who rant on street corners, Inspector," Pauline said, chuckling.

Ramsay laughed, though there was little mirth in his voice. "My sorrow will pass, Miss Riddell. Ethel deserved better than this."

"She murdered someone, Inspector," Pauline protested.

Ramsay was silent for a moment, then said, "You forget,

I've known her since she was a child. She was so earnest, so hardworking. Always thinking of others, always caring for others, and yet getting so little in return."

"You could say the same of many people," Pauline replied. "It isn't enough to excuse murder."

"She was a woman of your kind, Miss Riddell," Ramsay continued, as though Pauline hadn't spoken. "She went to university and became an engineer when the country needed women to man the factories. She worked hard, did what was right and, when the war was over, was returned to being just another girl in the office."

"Still not making me change my mind, Inspector," Pauline said. "Everyone makes sacrifices, and we don't kill people when we do -- and certainly not the people who tried to help us."

Ramsay laughed, but the sadness remained in his voice. "I agree that murder is murder and must be punished. However, I will say again, I knew her as a child. She deserved better."

Pauline nodded, though Ramsay couldn't see. That at least they could agree on. Stephen didn't deserve to die in a war on the other side of the planet over who should govern a country no one here had any right to decide on -- and yet he was dead. Like Ethel, Stephen had deserved better.

"I find, Inspector, that sometimes the result of a successful case isn't as satisfying as I'd like it to be."

This time Ramsay did laugh. "I would only add to that: most times the result is satisfactory, and some nasty people are rightly punished. This time isn't quite one of those, but we should still celebrate another success."

"I'm in meetings all the rest of the day," Pauline replied. "As you can imagine, there are to be changes here at the factory. Perhaps we could meet this evening?"

Pauline sipped her sherry while Ramsay sipped his pint of Tennants bitter. They sat side by side in companionable silence, monopolizing the Snug of the *Seven Stars*, a place mutually agreed on because it was unlikely anyone they knew would see them there. Their moods were equally low, and it was hard for them to look each other in the face. Instead, they gazed across the room to a hunting scene hanging on the wall. Even that seemed somber, morbid tonight.

It was some time before Pauline asked, "Have you an interesting case to begin on, now this one is finished?"

Ramsay shook his head. "For you, this one is finished. For me there's still the gathering of evidence for the Prosecution lawyer's case. That will take days, maybe weeks. Meanwhile, somewhere in the city another tragedy will occur, and I'll get to pick through more personal wreckage to find justice for someone who has been buried in the rubble."

Pauline laughed. "You make it sound like an apocalypse."

"For the person hurt by the tragedy, it will feel that way," Ramsay replied, smiling sadly. "Meanwhile it's just paperwork for me -- boring but not painful. And you?"

"I'm back to auditing," Pauline replied, "and I don't know how I feel about that. The past week has re-awakened my love of investigating and made me dissatisfied with my professional career."

"You managed our earlier collaborations while working, and now you've managed this one," Ramsay pointed out. "It doesn't have to be one or the other."

Pauline squirmed a little before saying, "That's why I

hoped you might have a new case where an amateur could help."

"It's more than my job is worth to bring in amateur assistance," Ramsay replied gravely. "Putting a member of the public in danger by co-opting them onto an investigation would be the end of me with the police force."

Pauline nodded. She'd expected exactly this response, but it was still disappointing. "I understand," she murmured.

"Of course," Ramsay continued, "we often use outside professionals when it's within their purview. Financial wrongdoing is a steady part of our business, if I can call it a business." He took another sip of his beer.

"I would charge if you're using my professional qualifications," Pauline remarked.

"Naturally. In fact, I couldn't use your expertise if you weren't being properly employed by the force," Ramsay replied.

"It seems I need to form a business," Pauline said. "How often might this happen?"

"Hard to say," Ramsay replied. "Not every case involves finance, and not every case that does comes to me."

"They might, if this case ends successfully," Pauline reminded him. "Maybe you could use it to ensure that all financial cases come your way in the future."

"I thought that too," Ramsay said. "Our financial experts have found no bigger anomalies and will likely leave your company alone for a time. Your boss may be safe and, if so, you should be as well."

"That is good news," Pauline replied. "Maybe I should start my business anyway, in case they suddenly find something and I'm suddenly unemployed."

"It's always useful to have a lifeboat to jump into,"

Ramsay agreed, chuckling. "Especially when it offers new opportunities in the future."

Pauline nodded and sipped her sherry. They returned to their quiet staring at the gaudy wallpaper of the room, a mass of deep red scrolls on a golden background. It had a nice Victorian feel to it, and Pauline found it surprisingly comforting in a world stacked high with nuclear bombs and an orbiting Sputnik overhead watching everyone. When contemplating leaping into an exciting, maybe dangerous, future, it was good to have a solid foundation from which to jump.

Also by P.C. James

Stay up to date with Miss Riddell Cozy Mysteries

vinci-books.com/MissRiddellCozyMystery

About the Author

I've always loved mysteries, especially those involving Agatha Christie's Miss Marple. Perhaps because Miss Marple reminds me of my aunts when I was growing up. But Agatha never told us much about Miss Marple's earlier life. While writing my own elderly super-sleuth series, I'm tracing her career from the start. As you'll see, if you follow the Miss Riddell Cozy Mysteries series.

However, this is my Bio, not Miss Riddell's, so here goes with all you need to know about me: After retiring, I became a writer and when I'm not feverishly typing on my laptop, you'll find me running, cycling, walking, and taking wildlife photos wherever and whenever I can.

My cozy mystery series begins in northern England because that was my home growing up and that's also the home of so many great cozy mysteries. Stay with me though because Miss Riddell loves to travel as much as I do and the stories will take us to the many different places around the world I've lived in or visited.